P9-ECC-905

TAKIN' IT BACK

TAKIN' IT BACK

John A Kuri

SEVEN LOCKS PRESS
SANTA ANA, CA

For permission requests, write to the publisher, addressed
"Attention: Permissions Coordinator," at the address below.

Seven Locks Press

P.O. Box 25689

Santa Ana, CA 92799

800-354-5348

Printed in the United States of America

ISBN 1-931643-69-5

Library of Congress Cataloging-in-Publication Data available on request.

Cover design: Christoph Klotz

Book interior design: Richard Cheverton/ Waypoint

For Mom and Dad,
    Eternally

And, to the ones who inspired this: Janiene, John, Jason, Jay, Alyssum, Alex, and
    Justin. Being lucky enough to watch you all achieve has given life greater
    meaning.

Author's acknowledgment

Success has many parents, yet failure is an orphan. In the pragmatist's view, success will be measured in sales. But measurements at that point are well after the fact for the believers, since they chose to risk their time, effort, or resources.

In the instance of this novel, there are certain individuals, who without any guarantees, have taken a position in support of the purpose this story serves. Standing at my side and shepherding this project has been Douglas Gorman. His insight has been brilliant, his dedication inexorable.

And there are many to whom I owe a debt of gratitude. In a variety of ways, they have helped champion the project, and in doing that they each have helped give life to *Takin' It Back*. They include: Douglas Kruse, Dr. David Kuri, Feturah Miller, John Daric, Russ Tinsley, Anita Coolidge, Sieglinde Schmidt, Rick Buhay, Kurt Meyers, Gene Hubert, Eric Maryanov, Alan Nunner, Jeff Kennedy, Chris Verdugo, Stephen Enkeboll, and James Riordan.

Contents

Foreword . . . .*xi*

Prologue . . . .*xv*

Preface . . . .*xxiii*

1.   Fo'Shizzle 1
2.   One Kind Favor 8
3.   Jesus Juice 12
4.   A Penelope 14
5.   187 17
6.   A Hard Life And Then... You Get To Die 22
7.   Smack 24
8.   Where It All Begins 29
9.   Alyssum 34
10. There's Danger On The Edge 36
11. Them That Do, Them That Don't 41
12. A Farewell in Blue 45
13. Hoops Without Art 48
14. Takin' Back the 'Hood .52
15. A Hottie 56
16. Poppi 59
17. Floating The Lure 62
18. A Journey Begins With the First Step 69
19. Finding Words 83
20. Where He Left Off 86
21. Come to My Office 92
22. Bringing Home the Laundry 96

23.   Reaching Out 102

24.   Price of Fame 110

25.   Alone 115

26.   Wandering Eyes 120

27.   It's My Pain 124

28.   Life's Over 127

29.   Inside 131

30.   Please Mom 136

31.   One Step Forward 142

32.   Two Steps Back 148

33.   Aces & 8s 149

34.   Thin Air 152

35.   Yes! We Are 165

36.   Teamwork, Fools! 170

37.   A New Life 173

38.   Death Gives Life 179

39.   The Game 183

FOREWORD

What we read should be thought-provoking, as well as interesting. We should all have some sense of responsibility to the words that are collected from the pages, because if we do just that, we will be changed in some manner or another: outwardly or inwardly.

Every once in a while a book comes along that causes the reader to yearn, or warrants the reader to want to reach deeper than just seeing white pages with writing on them. This book epitomizes the impulse. I myself was very moved by this story and how well it parallels so many of our lives, in a personal way. We sometimes go through life thinking that we have nowhere to turn for answers. Some think that life's problems are solved by values. For me, this book proves that through compassion and dedication, people can change, and perceptions can change too.

Also, this story exemplifies the fact that people are truly good-natured and do care what happens to our youth of today's society. As much as we attempt to look the other way, our compassion for our children seems to rise to the top, more than ever. It makes us want to care more and embrace the kids, to help them see that they can make a change in their lives. John Kuri has captured this human phenomenon in its full essence within this novel. This is a story that is not only to be read personally, but shared and talked about with others, near and far. It's also a feel-good story, for those who already have engulfed themselves in similar situations or projects. John recognizes these people in his story. Legacy will be passed forward in print through this book.

Often we find solace through others to rectify our own problems. This story follows this pattern somewhat. We need other people in our lives, companionship to develop ideas about the way we handle our everyday problems.

We often search for different answers throughout what we hear other people voice in conversation. This story shows that through sacrifice, patience, and kindness, lives can change—and will change. It only takes a few concerned people to alter patterns of bad behavior. And there are points, in young lives especially, when it may be impossible to imagine that someone you have hurt just might turn around and help you change from bad apple to a keeper.

One man's dream of hope for a neighborhood kid can be a dream of hope for the world. We are all capable of lending a strong positive hand to the youth of today. Let them know that there are important people who truly care what happens to them now, and in the future.

In a world where there is so much negativity toward our young people, John Kuri depicts another man's dream for our youth through his story. Knowing John, I truly sense this is his dream for our youth today. In this novel he so graciously depicts each scene so that the reader feels what he felt when he was writing it, or in some instances, perhaps living it.

When reading the manuscript, I felt very much a part of the story. I grew up in a similar situation. I've seen kids in my travels with these problems, with seemingly nowhere to turn. I've seen them find their way, and come out ahead with just a touch from a loving voice, or a gentle push in the right direction. It's truly a blessing that we have John to constantly remind us, through his writing, what is important in our society.

Hopefully, you will read this book with great admiration and heart-provoking thoughts.

Enjoy!

Jerome Kersey

Authors's Note: Mr. Kersey won his NBA championship ring while playing for the San Antonio Spurs in the 1999 National Basketball Association world championship games. He played in the NBA for seventeen years on teams including the Los Angeles Lakers, Portland Trailblazers, Seattle Sonics, Golden State Warriors, Milwaukee Bucks, and San Antonio.

Currently, he is an assistant coach with the Milwaukee Bucks.

PROLOGUE

The future belongs to the kids. In fact, what I have observed during my transitions through life is, once past the mid-twenties every changing trend is about the next generation—of consumers. That's right. The little guy lost in his Sony PlayStation console is being groomed, his taste buds are being developed, for soon he'll be an iPod buyer, and then he'll be seeking a cellphone, a BlackBerry®, and eventually, every high-end toy imaginable.

Mass marketing has changed the way kids grow up, and that is largely because of advances in technology. First it was television. Its impact struck my generation in the days when calling a girl who was a sixth-grade classmate meant getting permission to use the family phone. The black-and-white picture tube drove sales of Davy Crockett coonskin caps and the records that were first spun on Dick Clark's "American Bandstand." Elvis and his hips, the Beatles and their hair? It all was marketing directed at the youth, and it came racing into homes by way of television.

The next huge landmark was the MTV generation. It found its beginning when I was raising my kids. From Madonna to Nirvana to U2 and Depeche Mode, MTV brought music videos into the home, again by way of television. The computer was becoming a household word about that time, and learning to use it became a mandate for the future. For the kids, computer language was akin to playing games. After all, how different was it for an eight-year-old to figure out Pac-Man versus a computer that also had games? Not much.

Then the digital revolution, along with the Internet, landed on the planet and once again everything we thought was state of the art was yesterday's news. Our analog way of life gave way to random access of just about anything we could imagine. Cassette players or the already antiquated eight-track player were relegated to the trash heap. And the cellphone, through wireless technology, would change everything. Kids now carry cellphones, or if they don't, they are explaining to their parents how to program them. Everyone, it seems, is hooked together in a wireless world.

Writing about changes in technology is not the purpose of Takin' It Back. These opening words are here to bring to mind how fast time brings changes that impact our lives. Sitting down to dinner with mom, dad, brothers and sisters is now a quaint concept. No one has time for old-school traditions. Single-parent families have become a way of life in America. A lot of people are just trying to survive. Some are trying to make better lives for themselves and their kids. Growing divorce rates and childbearing out of wedlock, is common in the North, South, East and West, and has led to a prevalent circumstance of less direct parental involvement.

Meanwhile, here come more kids, and many of them don't know who their fathers are. The ones lucky enough to be born into homes with educated parents have a chance at getting through the morass that lies ahead of them. While educated parents may not guarantee a better childhood environment, a child having that benefit is perceived to have an advantage. Those who live in unstructured homes, and those who are poor, have a world of odds stacked against them before they are ever weaned. In some studies, including the 2000 U.S. Census, the source of the data provided below, kids in the later circumstance are classified as "at risk."

In this country at the beginning of the 1970s the number of single parent-families with children younger than eighteen was 3.8 million; by 1996 the number had more than quadrupled to eighteen million. Now, one in four children is born to unmarried females, usually teenagers. By 1992, 68 percent of African American babies were born to unmarried females.

Why is it that the smartest minds in advertising and marketing realize that the future of the companies they represent, design new sales concepts and mastermind the spending of billions of dollars annually, are so aware that the future is in the kids? But at the same time, why is a large percentage of kids ignored as a part of a landscape many adults don't wish to traverse? I am referring to the 5.6 million at-risk kids who basically have little access to the opportunities our culture offers. Many are left only to their dreams.

The 2000 Census gave cause for many people to rejoice in the news that there had actually been a decrease in the number of children living in high-poverty neighborhoods. Some in the political ranks have leaned on that news, which on the surface feels good. But peeling back the first layer of information and reading the more comprehensive measure of neighborhood quality, one realizes that severely distressed neighborhoods are the home to a growing number of at-risk children.

In fact, despite the booming 1990s economy, the number of children living under such distress increased 18 percent, from 4.7 million in 1990 to 5.6 million in 2000. In that time frame, the number of adults in those neighborhoods grew from 10.4 million to 12.5 million, a 20 percent increase.

The numbers broken down show that of the 5.6 million kids, 55 percent are black and 29 percent are Hispanic. Or, 28 percent of all black children live in severely distressed neighborhoods, and more than 13 percent of all Hispanic children face the same circumstance.

A severely distressed neighborhood is defined as one that has three of the following four characteristics: High poverty rate (27.4 percent or greater); high percentage of female-headed families (37.1 percent or more); high percentage of high school dropouts (23 percent or more); high percentage of working-age males not in the labor force (34 percent or greater).

Kids growing up in this circumstance, and again, that's 5.6 million in number, largely black or Hispanic, represent a huge segment of the future of this country. To this writer, they live in the most vulnerable conditions; they have little chance of finding their way to a life with any promise of quality. It should be noted that black and Hispanic kids together comprise about one-third of all the kids in the United States.

This information is shouting a loud and clear message: There is an enormous gap between mainstream society and a significant segment of the minority community. That gap will somehow have a life of its own as the next decade or two pass, and will very probably take a huge toll on society as we now know it. Deny some kids the structure of a family; leave them to a public education system within the innercities, acknowleged to be in trouble; give them idle time on the streets; and the disparity between their class and others probably widens. What will manifest in those same kids is a have and have-not perception.

Those at-risk kids may be drawn to the web of the drug or gang culture. Education and its value as a means to support a life, or raise ones' standard of living, is a difficult concept to sell to a teen who has seen easy money through crime, or felt a sense of glamour and power offered through an underground, anti-mainstream culture. Some become wards of the state, some find their way to the morgue. There are the few of the at-risk kids drawn in a positive direction through the guidance and counsel of a mentor—be they a teacher, athletic coach, volunteer, or family member.

Technology has changed much of the way we live. But there remains a constant need that technology can only partially address: communication. People need contact with people. And kids need family, in whatever form they can get it. The traditional mom or dad relationship to the child, whether adolescent or teen, is a human fundamental. Beyond the structure of a home, the discipline and authority of a parent, is the issue of the mentor—the person who can share the life lessons that cannot be learned in the classroom. It is this part of a child's world that this fact-based novel focuses on.

The story told here brings off-duty Los Angeles police officers together with young teen boys on city playground basketball courts. The officers mentor the boys in the sport, teaching them the value of team effort and discipline, showing these young minds that they can aspire to something bigger than the world they inhabit.

The national organization PAL (Police Activities League or Police Athletics League) has 370 chapters in cities across the country. They are served through the efforts of off-duty officers who give of themselves to over two million at-risk kids in their communities.

The executive board of Hollywood PAL, like those of all PAL chapters, is made up members of the community and representatives of law enforcement. It is the cooperative effort of these citizens that is making a difference in the lives of youths from less-privileged homes. The youths are potential victims of the gangs that inhabit the streets and shadows around the playgrounds. In Takin' It Back the volunteers, with the cooperation of the LAPD and its off-duty officers, get actively involved with the vulnerable at-risk teens—just as in real life.

The novel pays tribute to fallen officers, their lives having been taken by teenage gang members. From the 2004 death of California Highway Patrol Officer Thomas Steiner, gunned down by a sixteen-year-old boy wanting to impress the 12th Street Gang of Los Angeles County's San Gabriel Valley, to a similar event two decades ago in Chicago, to fallen LAPD officers Filberto H. Cuesta Jr. and Steven Gerald Gajda, both killed by gang members in 1998, this story is about life and death. Will kids living in the impoverished parts of cities have a chance at life or are they dead on arrival?

This is also about the real people who want to give back to their cities and be a part of change, lighting the candle rather than cursing the darkness. Characters such as the fictional Sanchez, a store owner who mentors one of the boys, typical of the PAL board members; or the fictional Detective Danny Smith, a veteran Robbery/Homicide supervisor who deals with the reality of the streets but struggles with how to reach his own teenage son.

LAPD Commander Michael Downing, an internationally respected law enforcement officer, is a veteran who inspired the Danny Smith character. He is a proud father of two, active in coaching his daughter's softball and soccer teams. In addition to his intense professional life and his devotion to his family, Mike has been an active part of Hollywood PAL, serving on its executive board as a senior advisor from the LAPD.

The novel's Kathy Montalvo, formerly a college basketball star and now an LAPD officer, decides in her off-duty hours to take on the challenge of coaching five teenage boys in memory of an assassinated officer, Art Jackson. He was a mentor coaching playground basketball and was killed off-duty, on the same courts where he had coached the five teens on so many afternoons.

The real-life embodiment of Kathy is Captain Anita Ortega of the LAPD. She was a UCLA All Star, playing on the school's women's basketball team, and was the leading UCLA scorer in the final 1978 NCAA championship game. She is also a member of UCLA's and the LAPD's Hall of Fame. At 27 she decided to join the LAPD as a way of giving back. During her twenty-year career, she has worked everything from traffic to narcotics and has risen in rank to the position of a patrol division commanding officer. However, Anita finds time to officiate Division 1 women's basketball, all this while being mom to her adopted daughter, Mia.

Jerome Kersey, former NBA star and current assistant coach of the Milwaukee Bucks, is another of the real-life inspirations behind Takin' It Back. He has participated with the PAL chapter in Portland, Oregon, and was a mentor for young players drafted by the Portland Trailblazers during his final years on staff with that team.

Rob Koplin, Hollywood PAL's executive director, is another believer in the effort of these selfless mentors. His eternally optimistic outlook drives his spirit and thus his contributions to the PAL kids.

These real people share a value: They know that the kids are our future. It struck me recently that for adults, Andy Warhol's suggestion of fifteen minutes of fame has long since passed. It did when we were too young to notice, too inexperienced to realize. But now is the moment to believe firmly that anything done to positively affect young lives can only carry an innately beneficial effect to the future of this country. The kids have yet to be given their fifteen minutes.

Each day the off-duty police officers of PAL like Commander Downing and Captain Ortega, the NBA stars like Jerome Kersey who have made the choice to mentor, moms and dads, big brothers and sisters, and countless organizations and their army of volunteers, are giving back. This book is in part about their selfless efforts.

Mostly, this novel is about all kids, like mine and yours, and the ones you see any day of the week hanging around playgrounds. They look you in the eyes and ask the questions whose answers cannot be found in books. Teenagers challenge the best of the best in ways adults could not imagine. I did it to my parents and fortunately for me they did not give up. My kids did it to me, and their kids will challenge them. Along the way we can only hope to stay with our kids in the game of life, and that out there on those streets they walk each day, they will find the positive opportunity of their lives rather than the negative alternative.

PREFACE

Graffiti is the art of the streets. Some is created by a single "tagger," some by "crews." All of it is a part of the hip-hop culture. If we were living in ancient Egypt, we would call it hieroglyphics. Spray paint cans are the brushes, and buildings, signs, bus benches, buses, and trash receptacles are the canvases. To some, it is the work of twenty-first-century Picassos.

A "piece" is a pictorial representation specific to the tagger. In street vernacular, a piece (short for "masterpiece") is a mural—elaborate and large in scale using a wide palette of colors. Piecing is the pinnacle, and contemporary art connoisseurs recognize the piece as an expression of the culture, raising the tagger's work from vandalism to gift.

Hip-hop culture is global. From El Locomoco and Alamo City hip-hop in San Antonio, Texas; to the South Bronx; to Melbourne, Australia; to the Hifi art in San Francisco; the Graffito in Milano, Italy; to the work of the L.A. crews, seen in many parts of the sprawling Southland, the hip-hop culture speaks of the social landscape.

Rap is a part of Hip-Hop. It is a musical form using storytelling lyrics that sometimes rhyme, accompanied by a synthesized rhythmic background beat. If you want to understand what's goin' down, listen. Ultimately, rap is "Urban CNN."

CHAPTER 1

FO'SHIZZLE

(for sure)

I t was a piece they passed each day, the tagger's statement of time and place painted on the otherwise lifeless brick that made up a thirties industrial building, now a pawn shop. John Paul and his best friend, Michael, never noticed the piece, its statement both anger and pain. The two boys, both fifteen, were heading to the playground basketball courts in the heart of Hollywood.

John Paul's black hands, with such long fingers, allowed him to palm the ball like his idol, Shaq. John Paul was Dominican, "JP" to his buddies. JP passed the ball to Michael, a handsome, tortured twenty-first-century James Dean. He could turn the charm on with a smile that evoked the confidence of someone older.

They moved with a rhythm all their own, graceful and smooth. The backdrop could have been a stage mural rather than trash cans and urban debris, the flooring could have been hand-laid hardwood rather than potholes, broken asphalt, and oil stains.

As they cleared the alley and moved up the Cahuenga Boulevard sidewalk alongside the city playground, they were within view of the not-so-distant and ever-so-famous "Hollywood" sign, a part of the Hollywood Hills landscape that is synonymous with the movie capital of the world. But to JP and Michael it had no more significance than the red CNN logo atop the Sunset Boulevard high-rise three blocks away. Yes, these boys lived in the heart of the dream capital, but it could as well have been Detroit, East St. Louis, or the Bronx.

In the '50s, the area a half-block south, across Santa Monica Boulevard, was home to the famous Technicolor film lab and other motion picture post-production optical and title houses. Those companies had moved away to newer industrial areas, leaving the relics of the past casting shadows across the park's baseball diamond. The residences in the area were a mixture of mid-'50s apartment buildings and '40s vintage houses. In its day it was a middle-class neighborhood, but that luster was only a memory. Over time as more people moved to the suburbs, this fringe inner-city area became home to low-income Hispanics, blacks, and a few whites.

The intense boom from the bass line in a rap song filled the street from a passing Oldsmobile 98, the most respected sedan of the hip-hop generation. JP and Michael crossed the street behind the passing car, dark eyes peering out from just above its doorframes. The boys moved along the chain-link playground perimeter toward the basketball courts. In a shady spot under a lone tree, a group of teens hung out, smoking pot and tossing down malt liquor.

In contrast to that brain-starving activity, the basketball court was filled with the athletic energy of a group of fifteen-year-olds. As JP stepped on the court to join his friends, he received a pass. He glanced away from the basket and passed the ball to Michael.

Alonzo, black, overweight, his haircut a fade, was known as Lonzo to his friends. He took Michael's pass and tried to move to his right against a boy named Dennis. But Lonzo's stride revealed a weakness on his left side. He was the son of an addict, and he paid a price for his mother's addiction with every step. Lonzo did his best to fake a shot, then passed back to Michael who was guarded by the very tall Sam, AKA High-top. Dennis, a loose-jointed black kid, not as tall as High-top, was playing defense with Sam and Anthony, a good-looking Puerto Rican-and-Mexican mix, known as "Tone."

All the boys wore basketball shorts that seemed a little large. It was a style thing. For Lonzo, it meant he was constantly adjusting his shorts under his belly. He liked to keep them right on his hips.

Art Jackson, a forty-five-year-old black man with a likable round face, coached these boys with intensity from the sideline. His signature unlit cigar was clenched in his mouth. His T-shirt sported a Los Angeles Police Department PAL insignia.

Art loved these boys like they were family. His wife, Heather, and he had been unable to have their own. The boys were an answer to Art's longtime desire to have a son. Put all the boys together and he saw only one color—innocence. But he knew each one was an individual ready to be shaped into a man. Left to the streets, they would likely be under one of those shady trees finding brotherhood with other lost teens, each one step from crime, or drugs, or the Grim Reaper.

Sports, basketball in particular, offered a language that bridged the otherwise broad chasm between the responsible adult police officer and the teens of this Hollywood neighborhood. So, as he had so many afternoons, cigar in mouth, Art watched the game played.

Sam was all over Michael, blocking his shot. Michael passed to JP to shake Sam loose. Then JP made his move and for a second got in front of Sam. JP drove forward from the top of the key, but as Sam closed in again JP passed to Michael at fifteen feet from the boards. Michael was anticipating the pass and immediately set and took his shot.

Sam's instinct was ahead of JP and Michael, though. He knew those two were almost inseparable in all things. And there was more than one reason he was called High-top. He timed his jump against the arch of the ball, watching as it traveled against the afternoon's hot blue sky. The ball spun in a rhythm that seemed connected to that constant rap that rolled across the grass from the congregated gangs.

Art, like an expectant father, stopped chewing on his cigar as he watched Sam starting his leap to block the shot. Art was so intense his eyes could make out each rotation of the ball. Then he saw Sam's hand move in as the ball spun toward the hoop, still in the upward arch. Sam blocked the shot.

Michael was deflated and frustrated. "Shit!"

Art had no favorite. He just wanted heads-up playing from all of them. He stepped in and complimented Sam. "Good D, High-top."

Sam was slappin' skins with Dennis and Tone as JP moved toward Michael.

JP was a steadying presence. "It's cool, Michael, it's cool."

Michael did not buy JP's attempt to placate him. He just shook his head and refused to look at the three defenders prancing in joy.

Art could smell the trouble."Okay! Okay! Listen up, all you fools."

The group settled down and closed in toward Art.

"Now, that was team playing. Good moves—all of you."

Michael snapped, "Would'a made the shot if I drove in the first time I had it, Coach!"

"No! You would'a made it if High-top hadn't blocked it," Art fired back.

Sam teased Michael. "You never had a chance. You know what I'm sayin', Road dog."

Dennis slapped skins with Sam again.

Michael insisted, "I would'a had it!"

Art was quickly tiring of the attitude. "Wanna play one on one, Michael? You can play pickup ball any time. Wanna be in this posse, do it my way."

The look from Michael that followed Art was more of a challenge. Art looked away before Michael would be forced to answer and then offered Michael some advice. "Dust the dirt off your shoulders, Michael. Remember the donkey that wouldn't give up when the farmer couldn't get him out of the well? Remember the story?

Alonzo blurted out, "The donkey fell in the well. When the farmer gave up and started throwing dirt in, to bury the donkey, that's when the donkey shook it off."

Art nodded. "That's right, Lonzo. The donkey shook the dirt off his shoulders and started stepping up as the dirt landed in the well, instead of letting himself get buried under the weight of it. That's the same thing you dudes can learn to do."

The story struck a positive note with Michael. JP caught Michael's look of acceptance and put out his palm. Michael slapped skins with him.

Art smiled, and looked pleased. "Now, keep thinkin' teamwork and you pansies might make it to the PAL statewide games next February," he said.

The boys mocked the idea, but Art read their response as self-doubt. He could see that they did not believe they could make it into those games. "You'll be steppin' over each other to get in line for the Southern Cal summer sports competition in Angeles Crest. It'll be sponsored by one of the big companies so there's gonna be lots of free gear for anyone who attends."

Alonzo jerked his head up. "Free?"

Art responded, "Yeah. Some of the teams from PAL chapters will be up there. So, why not you fools. And, it's sponsored. You knuckleheads know what that means?"

They all looked at him, waiting for the answer.

"That means you'll be coming home with new sneakers, shorts, shirts. And maybe there'll be some scouts there."

"Fo' shizzle?" Alonzo asked.

"Umh huh! Fo' shizzle," Art said, letting a grin slowly take over his face at the thought that he was speaking in Hip-hop.

Alonzo reacted first, and got so excited he began jumping up and down, his low riding shorts soon revealing his butt crack.

Art noticed and shook his head in disbelief. "Alonzo! What's with you and the shorts?"

Sam, a prankster, reached out and pulled Alonzo's shorts down, exposing his bare butt and lack of underwear.

Dennis pointed at Alonzo, "Ay yo trip!" Everyone looked.

Alonzo was embarrassed and pulled his shorts back up as the boys broke into laughter.

Alonzo turned to Sam, "Yo! Fool. Whadda ya doin'?"

Sam replied, "Freeballin' it, Lonzo? You know what I'm sayin'? Homeboy?"

Anthony added, "Flamboasting?"

Alonzo, less than happy to be the object of a joke, responded, "Shut your face."

Michael could not resist joining in, "Your grandma know you struttin' your stuff, Lonzo?"

Alonzo turned defensive. "No!"

Laughing so hard, Sam could barely get his words out.

Gasping, he said, "He puts his boxers on before he gets home, you know what I'm sayin'?"

The laughter was now out of control. Alonzo was so embarrassed all he could do was walk off. It pained Art to watch Alonzo knowing that each step on his left leg was an effort. But he also knew that Alonzo had to deal with things himself.

Art was overcome with the amusing sight as he called out, "Don't listen to these fools, Alonzo."

Without looking back, Alonzo waved them all off. After a few more steps, again without looking, he mooned them. And once again laughter took over the group. They watched as Alonzo disappeared up the street.

Art brought things back to the moment. "Okay. Tomorrow, same time, same place. Now, go straight home. I don't want to get any calls from your mothers."

CHAPTER 2

Art loved the blues. After a couple of hours on the playground courts, hearing the drive-by rap booming up and down the street, he loved turning on his car stereo loud enough to send a little of his music back. As he had explained to the boys before, the blues were here long before rap and would be here long after rap.

Art walked from the courts to his white Mustang convertible, his gear stowed in a large duffel bag. The car was parked fifty feet from the courts, curbside. He started up the engine. He loved listening to the throaty sound of its 4.6-liter V8 as he loaded the gear. But he also put on some blues. Today it was an early CD of legendary blues man John Hammond; the tune playing was Blind Lemon Jefferson's famous "One Kind Favor."

"One Kind Favor" had been performed by many artists. From the rock, folk, and blues worlds there were many interpretations. But there was something pure about this version that really appealed to Art. The fact that John Hammond is white was irrelevant to Art. What was crucial was John's soul, and Art heard that. Art was singing the lyrics as JP and Michael walked by the idling car.

"Well there's one kind favor I ask of you
Well there's one kind favor I ask of you
Lord it's one kind favor I ask of you
See that my grave is kept clean"

During a guitar riff Art looked up at JP and Michael walking by.

"Wanna ride? Get some pizza?"

Before JP answered Michael spun around and said, "Ain't got time."

The song's vocal began again and Art sang the verse without missing an inflection. He watched the boys walking on for a moment and then continued loading up his car while singing.

"It's a long lane, ain't got no end
It's a long lane, ain't got no end
It's a long lane, ain't got no end
And it's a bad wind that never came"

Art closed the trunk and watched the two boys as they crossed the street, that "Hollywood" sign sitting beyond them in the hills.

Art mumbled, "Someday, you'll learn to say thank you."

He mimicked the boys, "Thank you Officer Jackson." Then he laughed that infectious, deep and playful laugh of his.

As the vocal started again, Art continued singing.

"Lord there's two white horses in a line
Lord there's two white horses in a line
Lord there's two white horses in a line
Will take me to my burying ground"

As Art was about to get into his car, a basketball bounced toward him. He fielded the ball as a nineteen-year-old man, known as Crack, walked up. He was a hard-looking soul, black, had a scar curving down his right cheek, and dark eyes that said one thing—evil.

Art had seen Crack hanging around the courts before with his Souljas, an RTD bunch. Rough, tough, and dangerous was how they were known. To Art they were all losers and one of the reasons he chose to be there for his boys. No doubt these bangers dealt in drugs and whatever else could finance their lives.

Crack's eyes burned into the LAPD insignia on Art's T-shirt, a symbol that was polarizing.

On a rooftop of an old brick apartment building 100 yards down Cahuenga, a .30-06 bolt-action rifle took aim at Art. A sixteen-year-old black boy wearing a hoodie, was nervously lining up the shot. His Jheri-curls were poking out from the hood and his sleeves were shoved back revealing the forearm of his trigger hand. The hand had a distinctive tattoo: 18th Street for life. The lyrics of the tune coming from Art's car wafted through the night air into the shooter's sphere.

"My heart stopped beating, my hands are cold."

The teen's name was George Dupre, but he was "Smack" on the street. And this was going to be his first Jake, a policeman. George wanted a reputation. The idea of leaving the free world for life inside prison walls was a glamour thing in his shermed-out mind. He was into space-base: crack and angel dust mixed together for smoking. Tonight he would get respect from the 18th Street gang.

On the sidewalk Art tossed the ball to Crack, who did not change expression. Art grinned, saying, "Later, bro."

Crack ignored him and turned toward the court and his waiting posse. But his eyes glanced toward the rooftop. Did he know what George was about to do or was it just his nature to constantly look over his shoulder?

The lyrics continued and so did Art's singing.

"My heart stopped beating my hands are cold
Well my heart stopped beating, Lord my hands are cold
It was what the good book, Bible told."

Art was just at the driver's door as George said to himself, "Jake, you buyin' me some r'spect."

He squeezed off the shot. The rifle fired. The sound of the high-powered shot echoed from every building along the street. Art was slammed against his Mustang as the bullet struck him dead center in his chest.

At that same moment George dropped the rifle from the rooftop. It fell past windows clipping the fire escape as it made its way to the alley below. The wooden stock splintered on impact with the asphalt.

Art's suddenly lifeless body was now only supported by the car door. He was sliding to the cold concrete. His body came to rest, his face expressionless, his eyes still open. The song went into its last verse asking a final question to the now-silent Art.

"Have you ever heard that coffin sound
Have you ever heard that coffin sound
Have you ever heard that coffin sound
Did you know that poor boy neath the ground"

Crack was halfway to the courts as he summoned his crew. They casually moved off, disappearing in the shadows. Crack never looked back.

CHAPTER 3

Michael was moving at a good clip through the alley. JP was hustling to stay up with him.

JP popped Michael on the arm, "What you mean, you ain't got time for pizza?"

Michael responded, "Just what I said."

JP arched his neck, "But you got time to walk?"

Michael ignored his friend as they moved past an old car on jack-stands. They passed a pile of rubble on a lot next to an apartment building.

They crossed a residential street and entered an alley, passing a few drugged-out souls living amid debris. One of the alley residents, a weathered man in his mid-50s, was pouring some cheap Merlot into a Coke can when he noticed the boys. At that same moment, the distant sound of the .30-06 round that killed Art passed the alley. Gunshots were common, so no one reacted.

JP stopped with a look of panic across his face.

"Shit! She'll kill me!" he exclaimed.

Michael responded, "What? What?"

JP looked at him, true panic on his face. "My mother. I left my jacket at the court."

JP was running back through the alley before Michael could react.

Michael laughed. "She'll bust your ass if you're late."

Then he yelled, "You never gonna win, JP. Can't make none of 'em happy."

Michael turned to leave as the man with the Coke can approached him. His hands were unsteady, and his odor took the form of a dense and putrid wave that warned of his proximity.

Michael looked at him, unmoved by his destitute condition.

The old man tried to be friendly. "Say, young friend, got a smoke?"

Michael snapped back, "I ain't your friend, and get your Jesus juice breath outta my face!"

Michael moved off, leaving the old man to his world and words spoken that no one listened to.

The old man, speaking to the ether said, "That which dies is born." Michael, who had faded from view around the corner, did not hear him.

CHAPTER 4

A PENELOPE
(Female police officer)

Katrina "Kathy" Montalvo was in her late twenties. Her dad was Puerto Rican, and her mom was an African American from Mississippi. Kathy grew up in South Central Los Angeles, an area that became infamous during the Watts riots of 1965 and again during the Rodney King riots of 1992.

Her bright eyes searched Detective Danny Smith, a Robbery/Homicide supervisor, with intensity. She was in his office at the Hollywood Community Police Station for a job interview.

On his desk the only personal item was a picture of a boy at fourteen kneeling beside a proud German shepherd. Danny was fidgeting with an unopened pack of cigarettes as he scanned her file.

Kathy finally inquired, "Detective, do you need a light?"

"No. I quit," he replied without looking up, and put the cigarette pack in his pocket. Then he looked at Kathy.

"Explain to me why—why I want you as my partner?" he asked.

"'Cause I'm damn good at anything I do."

Danny cocked his head. "Why would you be interested in RHD, especially in this part of town?"

"As you can see, I've spent time in Central, Rampart, and Hollenbeck."

Danny seemed perplexed. "Yeah, and a lot of time in the communications division. Why the streets now?"

"That's where it's happening, right?" she responded.

Before he could answer her there was a knock at the door. Detective Charles Tyler, a well-dressed black man of thirty-five, opened the door and motioned to Danny. He had a scar on his right hand from a gunshot injury.

"Excuse me for a second," Danny said to Kathy. He crossed to the door. Waiting for him she noticed a commendation on his wall from the city of Los Angeles for meritorious service. Danny returned to his desk, completely distracted.

Danny looked at her for a moment and said, "I think you better come with me."

"Yes, sir," she responded.

Danny moved through the chaos of the squad room with Kathy on his heels.

At the same time, JP was backtracking to the playground. He had taken a shortcut that led him down the alley alongside the apartment building George used to sight in on Art.

JP was running when he came up on the rifle. There it was, in plain sight. He stopped and looked at the splintered weapon. It was a curious thing, he thought, obviously dropped from above. JP looked up, maybe expecting to see someone who had dropped the weapon. But no one was looking. He leaned over and picked it up.

Timing in life is everything. In this case it was really bad timing for JP. Just as he stood up with the rifle, a car penetrated the still of the alley. The bright headlight caught his attention. High beams burned his eyes as he looked. Then he made out the unmistakable silhouette of a police cruiser light bar. JP dropped the rifle and ran.

The police car came to a stop alongside the broken rifle, and an officer stepped from the car and identified the object.

"We've got a thirty-ought-6 here. Might be the weapon," he said.

His partner called in the discovery as the officer put on evidence gloves and picked up the weapon.

CHAPTER 5

187

In the California Penal Code, a 187 is a homicide. When a well-known, and in this case, loved police officer is the victim, the mood at the crime scene is noticeably different. A police officer is not just another victim; he is a fallen brother.

The media had heard the radio calls and arrived en masse. Strobe lights flashed from the perimeter of the yellow crime scene tape and illuminated Art's body from different angles. Overhead, a police Jet Ranger circled, its high intensity light filling the scene.

Alonzo was holding JP's jacket while taking in the scene with other spectators. He began to weep when seeing JP approach. JP began to understand what he was looking at and then tears began to drop on his cheeks.

A few feet away the officer from the alley spoke with Detective Tyler. He pointed toward JP and Alonzo.

Alonzo was looking at JP for answers. "He tolds us the hood trusted him, John Paul. Things was a'ight."

JP was staring at policemen, the news reporters, and Art's fallen body as the coroner began his investigation.

"Nothing a'ight, now," JP uttered.

A hand came down on JP's shoulder. It was Tyler.

"Boy! Over here, now," Tyler demanded.

"What?" JP questioned.

"I ask the questions. You wanna get along, shut your mouth."

Tyler, his hand firmly squeezing the back of JP's neck, led the frightened boy to an unmarked sedan. Alonzo trailed along, dragging his very tired left leg, but was waved off by the officer who had made the ID on JP.

At the car, Tyler spun John Paul around, pushing him against the door.

"You just came out of that alley?" the detective insisted.

JP said, "I didn't do nothin."

"That's not what I asked you, boy." And Tyler asked him again.

An unmarked car pulled up. Danny and Kathy got out and moved toward the crime scene. As Danny walked to Art's body, a criminalist stepped to his side and quietly spoke. He gave Danny a description of the wound, suspected caliber of the bullet, and approximate time of death.

Meanwhile, Tyler's interrogation of John Paul got Kathy's attention. She moved close enough to hear the exchange.

"You were in that alley!" Tyler charged.

"Yeah. So?" JP answered obstinately but also with fear. This man was nothing like Art, JP thought. Art would have never treated him this way.

Tyler cuffed JP. "You're going with me."

"For what?"

"You little asshole, you know for what."

"I don't know for what. I didn't do anything."

Tyler opened the rear door and roughly pushed him inside. "You're gonna tell me about the rifle, boy."

"I don't know nothing about it," JP insisted.

"Your fingerprints won't lie." Tyler slammed the door and walked off toward the crime scene.

JP and Alonzo made eye contact at that moment.

"I told 'em you didn't do nothing," Alonzo said to JP. He looked around, but knew none of these policemen would listen to him.

Kathy was watching Alonzo and approached him.

"Is he your friend?" she asked.

Alonzo began to cry. "Yes. He didn't do nothing."

"Were you with him?" Kathy asked.

"Art was our friend. We wouldn't hurt him. He took us for pizza, helped us with the moves, so's we'd get into the basketball competition. No way we gonna hurt Art."

At the crime scene, Danny was taking a last look at his friend. He reached down and took Art's hand for a moment. They had met twenty-two years earlier, at LAPD's academy. They graduated together and spent their first few years on patrol as partners. Art had gone off to work narcotics and most recently was a part of the anti-terrorist task group. Danny was having a hard time believing that after all of Art's dangerous assignments, his longtime friend died at a neighborhood playground. It was the worst day Danny had ever experienced.

After a few moments he rose and started back to his car. Tyler stopped him.

"Detective, I've got a juvy in custody. He was spotted in an alley across the street with a rifle in his hands." Tyler pointed toward the car with JP.

Danny looked at the car and saw Alonzo and Kathy.

"How old's the suspect?" Danny asked.

"I guess—seventeen. Probably a banger, part of a crew. I think he's the perp." Tyler was confident he had Art's killer.

"What's he got to say?" Danny asked.

"He's got momentary amnesia," Tyler quipped, "but he'll talk."

Then Danny saw Art's wife, Heather, walking toward the crime scene.

Danny turned back to Tyler. "Take him in and get prints, but don't book him till I get back."

Danny moved toward Heather to intercept her, and got to her just as she saw Art.

He stopped her short. "Heather, don't look at him like this."

She ignored Danny and pushed past him to Art, dropping to his side. Danny moved in alongside her, feeling completely helpless.

Heather, tears streaming, touched her man's face.

"I knew something was wrong when you didn't come home. You always call me, sugar, and now here you are. What happened? You promised this could never happen. You told me they loved you." Then she looked over to Danny. "He was their friend."

Danny put his arm around her and pulled her toward him. Anguish spilled out as she began to cry. She held onto Danny's lapels, looking into his eyes.

"Why? Why Art? He loved everybody."

"I don't know, sweetheart." Danny could say no more. How could he explain it? There was no logic, no rhyme, no reason. It was insanity, he thought.

A minute passed, and he helped Heather to her feet, slowly moving her to an unmarked unit. He turned to the officer at the car. "Take Mrs. Jackson home," he said. The officer opened the rear door and Art helped her in. "I'll check in with you later, Heather."

The scene became crowded with neighborhood faces watching the excitement. A cop was dead, right there. This was more exciting than watching reality TV or freeway car chases, they thought. And the blood was real. Some of the faces were pained because they knew Art. Some were curious and some excited.

Sam had heard the word on the street and was now standing next to Alonzo. They both looked totally lost as Art's body was loaded in the coroner's vehicle.

Danny was standing by the open door of his unit, talking on the police radio when Kathy walked up.

"Ten Lincoln ten-four. Twenty-one David transporting second suspect. We'll be ninety-eight in ten." Danny put down the radio mike and looked over to Kathy.

Showing no emotion, he said, "We've got a juvy gang banger in custody. They're putting a rush on the prints."

He opened the door and stepped in. She got in and barely had the door closed as he pulled away.

CHAPTER 6

A HARD LIFE AND THEN...
YOU GET TO DIE

anny stopped at the intersection of Santa Monica and Cahuenga for the red light. He pulled his pack of cigarettes out of his pocket, took one and lit it. Kathy wisely stayed quiet.

As the signal turned green, Danny hung a quick right. He took another drag trying to choke back the tears that were coming. Halfway down the block, Danny threw the cigarette out the window. He grabbed the pack and crushed it.

In a burst of emotion he hung another right onto Cole Avenue and stopped. Danny shut off the ignition and sat silently. Suddenly he hit the steering wheel hard with the bottom of his closed fist. He threw the door open and stepped out, into the traffic lane, almost being hit by a passing car. The driver honked, but Danny was oblivious as he walked to the back.

From the shotgun seat Kathy craned her head, watching him. Danny began kicking the rear bumper repeatedly, with increasing intensity. Again, Kathy knew to leave him be."God damn it!" he screamed.

Across the street an old woman was pushing a shopping cart up the sidewalk. She did not react to Danny's anguish. She had the look of a woman who had suffered plenty of her own, and she was more interested in safe passage along the sidewalk. She was passing a pair of teens lampin' mid-block. Lampin is a hip-hop term for hanging under a street light. Timing was on her side this evening because the teens were more interested in the police sedan across the street and Danny's anguish than the woman passing them.

After a few moments, Danny regained his composure and got back in the car. He looked over to Kathy but said nothing.

She asked, "You all right?"

He took a moment and nodded. Then he asked her, "You sure you want to do this?"

Without hesitation she responded, "Yes."

"Working in central communications is good. You help us, but you don't have to deal with the vermin directly." He watched her eyes, looking for any sign of doubt. "It's a hard life out here. Hell, it's a hard life for anyone. You work your ass off, some of us raise our kids, fight the good fight for them, for ourselves, and when it's all over, we get to die."

"I'm absolutely certain, Detective." Kathy didn't blink nor did she break contact with him.

"Okay, Detective Kathy Montalvo. You're hired."

Danny started the car and pulled out, heading north up the street. The teens watched from their turf, under the street lamp. And the old woman entered her humble dwelling, safe for the evening.

CHAPTER 7

SMACK

The Hollywood Community Police Station sits on ground long occupied by the LAPD. The old building had given way to a newer facility 20 years earlier. The fire department down the block was still housed in the classic structure built back in the '30s. The newer police division building had the usual industrial space design: cold colors and very utilitarian in its layout.

John Paul was in an interrogation room with Tyler. Panic to hatred ran through JP's face as his eyes followed his accuser.

"I know you're a banger. Where were ya taking the rifle, dick head?" Tyler was leaning into JP, trying to force a confession.

The room was a typical sterile green with a mirrored one-way window on the wall opposite John Paul. The boy was facing something that he was too young for, but that's the way of things today. Everything happens early. Kids can't be kids for long. JP was trying to be tough but he was clearly frightened.

"Answer me, boy. The sooner you do, the sooner you call your mama."

In a clone of this room, sixteen-year-old George sat with casual contempt, making no attempt to cover his 18th Street gang tattoo.

Kathy sat across from him, a rap sheet in her hands.

"George Dupre, you better be thinking about cooperating" . . . . . .

He interrupted her. Not only because she was female, but she was a Penelope. "Name's Smack."

She continued, with the raise of her eyebrows, "Whatever. This sheet on you—four, five years of arrests."

"I'm sixteen. You ain't messin' with my head."

Danny entered abruptly. He carried the rifle from the alley, an evidence tag tied to the trigger guard. Danny slammed it down on the table in front of George. Fingerprint dust was very apparent.

"Don't goddamn lie. The paraffin test, the prints. We have your ass." Danny waited for a response.

George cocked his head arrogantly.

"Let me tell you something, George, Smack, shithead, you're gonna be tried as an adult, for the cold-blooded murder of a police officer."

"Yeah, right," George responded while rolling his eyes.

Danny grabbed the rifle, shoving it in George's face.

"These are yours, fool."

George could not help but look at the prints.

After a moment Danny dropped the weapon.

"I wanna lawyer," George insisted.

Danny lunged, lifting George out of his chair and pressed him against the wall, his legs dangling on the chair seat. This scared George and Danny could see it. The veteran cop wanted this kid to confess. No Mr. Nice Guy since there was no doubt he was the perp. Kathy was concerned, not knowing how far Danny might go. Danny had not struck the suspect—yet, she realized.

"You're lucky you're not laid out at the coroner's," Danny said. Danny held him up for a moment and then dropped George into his chair.

Kathy interjected, "We've notified the juvenile authority. Someone is on their way here to represent you."

George pointed his tattooed hand at Danny. "I should'a picked you. Would'a gotten me in, just the same."

"What are you saying? You killed Art as a gang initiation?"

George fingered his tattoo, arrogance returning to his face.

In the other interrogation room, JP was still enduring Tyler.

"I don't know about the rifle," JP said again.

"Two of my guys saw you drop it, asshole."

A short-sleeved detective, Bill Wilson, rested against a steel-framed table, his arms folded across his belly. He was watching JP and Tyler through the window. Danny and Kathy entered. Danny and Wilson ignored each other as they looked on through the window at Tyler and JP.

"I told you. The rifle was lying there when I ran by," JP pleaded.

Wilson turned to Danny. "I told Tyler we had Art's shooter. But he thinks this kid knows something."

Tyler spun John Paul's chair toward him. "Okay. You wanna play?" Tyler thumped John Paul on the head.

Seeing that, Danny was out the door in a flash.

In the hallway Danny opened the interrogation room door and motioned to Tyler.

Tyler stepped into the hall and Danny got in his face. Kathy and Wilson had joined them in the hall, not wanting to miss what was about to happen.

"What the hell is happening in there?" Danny demanded.

Tyler, not unlike George, was arrogant. "What's the problem?"

"The suspect's in custody, confessed. You've been informed. Have you notified his parents that we detained him? And, what the hell are you doing with this kid, Tyler?"

"That little asshole knows something," he insisted.

"Tyler, he's going home. You handle a kid that way and I'll write you up, understand me?" Danny started for the interrogation room, but turned back to Tyler and continued.

"Assholes like you…" Danny stopped himself, knowing it was a waste of his time. Regardless of color there was prejudice to be encountered each day on the job, in one form or another.

Tyler pushed his way past Kathy and Wilson as Danny entered the interrogation room. Wilson turned to Kathy, extending his hand.

"New on the job?"

"Just transferred from downtown," she replied.

"Bill Wilson."

They shook hands.

"Kathy Montalvo."

He suddenly showed a devious grin. "Danny and Tyler. It's a love-hate thing."

That broke the tension and she smiled. It was a moment she appreciated from her newly discovered colleague.

Kathy entered the interrogation room, following Danny. He was seated opposite John Paul. The boy was still doing his best to show his mettle.

"What's your name, son?"

"John Paul. I told the other one, that's not my rifle."

"You do understand that your prints were on it," Danny said.

"I picked it up—but I wouldn't hurt Art. He was my friend."

"I believe you, son. Come on. My partner and I will take you home."

Relief overcame John Paul as fear and pain suddenly gushed.

"Did they take Art to the hospital? Is he coming back?" John Paul was pleading as much as inquiring.

Danny took a deep breath, containing himself before he could find a way to answer.

"I'm sorry, John Paul. Art isn't coming back."

John Paul began to weep. If Danny had said "Your dad's dead," it would have had less impact. This young man did not even know his dad. Art was the only male figure JP had ever known, that cared about him. Danny moved beside the teen, tenderly rubbing his back.

CHAPTER 8

Michael sat alone in the messy apartment. The furniture was shabby, not only from wear: It was cheap from day one. But this was the home of someone who had stopped caring, so it spoke of something greater than poverty itself. The TV offered the only light in the room. He was sitting in the combo living room, dining room, and his bedroom. This was a one-bedroom apartment in one of those buildings constructed during a real estate apartment boom in the early '60s. It was unlikely anything had been done to upgrade this relic.

Michael heard stumbling footsteps coming down the short hallway that led to the bedroom and the bath. His mother, Alicia Ahern, appeared wearing a tattered robe. She was unsteady on her feet, an all-too familiar condition.

In her day she was no doubt a beauty. Of Irish heritage, her fair skin that once glowed in sunlight was now almost lifeless and colorless.

"Hey, sugar, when you come in?" Alicia's eyes were dancing around the room looking for something. Michael could see this and it annoyed him.

"Nine. How come you're not at work?" he asked.

She stumbled forward still searching the room and asked, "You seen my purse?"

Michael walked to the breakfast table, picked up the purse from the chair and offered it to her. As she reached for it, her robe belt untied and dropped. She only had panties on and that was more than Michael wanted to know.

"Thanks," she offered.

Michael turned on a light as she searched her purse. She came out with a crumpled cigarette, then looked for a match. Michael picked up a book of matches, struck one and offered the flame to her. She took a big drag, unsteadily looking at him. She pulled him close for a hug.

"My little man, growing up so fast."

Her breath caused him to turn his face away, but he kept his eyes on her.

"What're you lookin' at?" she asked.

"Nothin'."

Alicia reclaimed her authority suddenly as she added, "Don't make a mess. I got enough to do without cleaning up for you."

As Alicia started back to the bedroom, she felt his stare burning in her back.

"You ain't much proud of me. Well, I'm doing the best I know how," she said, holding the wall for support.

"Mom, you can't drink so much. You promised this time you'd..."

She cut him off. "When you're paying the bills, maybe you can lecture me."

Michael was fighting back the tears. At that point he bolted out the door.

Michael stood at a freshly painted apartment door. It opened to a grandmotherly black woman, Mrs. Jones. She was nicely dressed, proud, and had kind but wise eyes. Michael was a pathetic sight for this woman to behold.

"Hi, Mrs. Jones. Is Alonzo here?" he asked.

"He's studying, which is what you should be doing." After a moment she said, "Well Michael, come in before you catch your death."

Michael stepped into a very clean, well-scrubbed home. The religious icons on display said it all. Alonzo came down the hall, looking low.

"Yo, Michael." The boys slapped skins.

"Your mother working late?" Mrs. Jones inquired.

"Yeah," he said, but she had reason to doubt his answer.

"Come in the kitchen," she said. "I'll fix you a plate."

Mrs. Jones went to the kitchen and as soon as she was out of sight Alonzo blurted out the news.

"Ay yo, trip. It's Art. Some 36-chambers did him. Jakes scooped up JP."

Michael was stunned. "What do you mean? Art's been shot? And what's the JP thing about?"

Alonzo was tearing up. "I dunno."

Danny, Kathy and John Paul were standing at the door of an appealing small home. It was a little Hollywood bungalow, painted white with a picket fence lining the sidewalk. John Paul's mother, Virginia Viasco, was a very attractive woman of Dominican descent. In her mid-thirties, she was dressed in a business suit. She was looking at her boy with keen eyes.

"These two arrested you?" she asked.

"No, Mom, another one. Asked me over and over about the rifle," he replied.

Danny wanted to explain. "Your boy was seen in the alley where the murder weapon was found. It was necessary to ask him some questions."

Virginia turned to John Paul. "You—get inside."

He hesitated, and she reacted immediately. "Homework! Now! No arguing."

JP went inside and Virginia pulled the door partially closed.

"And what did you find out, from your questions? The one's my boy was arrested for?" Virginia asked.

On any given day Virginia had intense eyes that told anyone she came in contact with that she was a seriously focused person. Danny read that immediately and was thinking about how to escape this encounter without losing too much of his hide.

"We have a suspect in custody now. Your boy wasn't involved." As he said it, he knew this last piece of information was correctly assumed by her.

She responded. "I could'a told you that. And if you spent more time preventing crime you wouldn't be needing to arrest boys like mine."

Before Danny could react Kathy jumped in. As she did he winced to himself.

Kathy offered, "If more parents were like you, we wouldn't have the problems we have."

"You just scared the shit out of my boy. Don't try to soften me up with your righteous judgment."

Kathy quickly fired back. "I don't pass judgment but I have had experience…"

At that point, without even looking at Virginia's face, which was turning purple, Danny knew this was no longer conversation. The exchange had gone from bad to horrible in two seconds flat. Danny thought Kathy may have set a land-speed record for provoking flash anger, as he took a half-step back.

"Experience!" exclaimed Virginia, her hands now placed on her hips.

"Easy now, ladies." But Danny knew it was too late.

"From your privileged middle-class point of view? Listen, girl, while I'm fighting my way up in this world, trying to make life better for my kid, I don't need your experience preached at my doorstep."

Kathy did not wince. "Really?"

Virginia added, "What the hell do you know about the life we live? And what the hell do you know about raising my son?"

Kathy was polite, but she showed an immediate strength that Danny never would have guessed.

"Mrs. Viasco, I grew up in South Central, worked my way out of it, no doubt like you may have. I look at life as a privilege. Every breath of it."

Virginia realized that those dark eyes locked on hers knew from where they had come. She grabbed the door handle. "Now, I won't be thanking you for bringing my boy home because you shouldn't have taken him in the first place. Good night."

Virginia stepped in the house, firmly closing the door.

"Community relations. Perfect job for you," Danny said.

As they walked toward the car, Danny's pager beeped. He looked down at the number, and there was a subtle change in his expression.

CHAPTER 9

The subway in Los Angeles primarily runs from downtown, in the central part of the city near City Hall, north through Hollywood and out to the eastern edge of the San Fernando Valley in North Hollywood. To understand the way the city was built one needed to know how it expanded decade after decade into a sprawling mass of humanity with suburbia giving way to growth and a constant influx of people wanting to call the City of the Angels their home. More suburbia kept developing on the perimeter of what was already supposed to be the end of the growth, so one can see that the subway system was a true afterthought born from absolute necessity.

Spend fifteen minutes on the 101 Freeway heading north or south out of downtown, virtually anytime, any day, and the picture will be as clear as the congestion of taillights seen in all lanes.

Michael was racing down a subway station staircase. The sound of the train stopping one level below was echoing off the tile walls. Above him a contemporary sculpture that only art students would ever look at was floating.

As Michael rounded a corner at the top of the last set of steps, he ran into two teenage girls, knocking the book bag from the hands of the prettier of the two. He would later discover that her name was Alyssum, like the flower. She was a very natural-looking sixteen-year-old with an unaffected persona and was dressed in a sporty choice of wardrobe.

Embarrassed, Michael immediately got down and began helping

her pick up the contents of the bag. In all the confusion, he had not looked at her. But as he handed her what he had retrieved, he was completely struck with her wonderful face.

"Sorry." Still dumbstruck, that was all he could think to say.

She was sweet and agreeable. "It's okay. I should'a been looking."

After a few seconds they rose to their feet in unison. The train alarm sounded its warning. Michael turned and ran, just making it onboard as the doors closed. Inside the doors, as the train pulled away, he watched her as she slowly walked away.

Alyssum looked back over her shoulder at him just as the train entered the tunnel.

Michael lost sight of her as passing red lights on the tunnel wall began to blur with the acceleration of the train. The lights became mesmerizing along with sound of the steel wheels rolling over the steel track.

CHAPTER 10

Danny's Explorer pulled out of the driveway of the West Hollywood sheriff's station. This was not LAPD patrol territory even though bounded by the City of Los Angeles on three sides. It was L.A. County. The sheriff's department had responsibility for the operation of the county jails all across the L.A. metro area, whether designated city or county.

Danny's very thin and tall nineteen-year-old son, Chris, was riding with him. He had been arrested for a DUI.

"If you thought I would use my badge to save your butt, well, son, think again."

"I was drinking, not sellin'."

Danny was really pissed. He had been down a road with his boy that seemed to have no exit, just a never-ending circle that held no evident purpose since no progress could be measured.

Danny and Chris' mother were divorced. There was plenty of guilt that gripped Danny every time he attempted to communicate with his boy. Her liberal methods of disciplining their son had been a source of his irritation to Danny for years. He wanted her to step up to the plate when the going was tough. Somehow she always had excuses or answers that seemed to come out of one of those textbooks she based her psychology lectures on.

"Why didn't you call your mother?" Danny asked.

"I'll get the bail money back to you."

"How? Finally getting a job?" Danny was exasperated enough to not hold back, his normal tendency.

The Explorer rounded a corner by a park and Danny stopped at the intersection.

"Thanks for coming, Dad, but I'll walk."

Chris hopped out and walked to the center of the park with no hesitation. Danny watched him while waiting on the traffic. He found a clearing and quickly parked.

Chris was lighting a Marlboro Red as Danny caught up to him.

"Chris. Life's a bitch. Why make it worse?"

Chris, who was totally enamored by Jim Morrison and the Doors, went into a weird space, reciting lyrics.

"Reaching your head to the cold, sudden fury, of a divine mess-en-ger." Chris stared at Danny. The look was a challenge. Danny did not take the bait.

The boy continued, "Waiting for the summer rain, there's danger on the edge of town."

"Trying to shock me?" Danny asked.

"Words from my soul."

"Why can't you get your life started and quit all the self-destructive crap?"

"What's the point?" Chris asked.

"It's being alive instead of being a stupid rock."

"So I can be a slave?"

Danny realized that Chris was not making a smart-ass teen comment, but the boy really saw adulthood in that light.

"Slaves? That's what you think life's about?" Danny was shaking his head.

Chris did not answer. He took a long drag off the cigarette instead, then responded. "Is this going to be one of those? You know, like when we sit down to eat and the questions start, and I get sick to my stomach."

Danny got up. This was another crucial moment in life. One of those teenage moments when there is no easy index card to reach for, no answer that handles the question. This was an inquiring mind, challenging the adult mind. This was his only kid and Danny spent each day trying to overcome his feelings of failure with parenthood.

Danny finally spoke what he thought was the simple truth about his relationship to Chris. "You don't talk to me. I have to ask the questions."

"You push."

"And I'll keep pushing for as long as it takes."

Chris started pacing, trying to contain his emotions.

Then he looked at his dad, straight on. "You know what I love about Poppi? He always has time. He never presses me. That's really cool."

"He's your grandfather. And he's getting older, so he's trying to slow life down because it's coming to an end."

Chris became defensive. "It isn't just because he's old."

Danny responded. "No. But it isn't his job to push. It's mine."

"I understand that. It's just all we talk about."

Danny justified. "The circumstances don't help."

"You threw me out." Chris was angry and hurt.

"Yeah! I did. I was hoping your mother, or school, a job, I don't care what. Anything that would influence you, lead you to do something with your music. Anything but hanging with your friends getting buzzed everyday, which seems to be your singular purpose right now."

With great sarcasm Chris agreed. "Right."

Danny was thinking better of what he said a second after the words were out of his mouth. With concern in his voice, he said, "You can do something with your life."

"Dad, why do you always try that positive shit with me?"

Danny did not hesitate. "You want to be negative, everything will look bad. Turn it around. Why slam your head against the wall, when you can walk around it?"

Chris just looked at him, not willing to take the step being offered. His eyes revealed his pain. After another moment Chris began again. "I remember when I was little. When you drank Mom didn't like it.

"So I drank a little too much."

Danny was not ready for what Chris said next. "Well, I'm just like you, Dad. I got your genes. I'm an alcoholic. I like to drink. It's the way I like life."

Danny almost laughed. But he stopped himself. His boy was speaking a truth, as he understood life from his very young view.

"You're not an alcoholic, son. You just started drinking, for Christ sake." Danny was shaking his head.

"Dad, hello? I started drinking when I was fourteen. I smoked my first bud at fifteen."

"Where?" Danny really wanted an answer.

"After school. In my bedroom sometimes, when you were passed out on the couch."

Danny became defensive. "I passed out watching football."

Chris gave him a look, and Danny knew Chris was not buying his line.

Danny continued, "Your mother left both of us. You blaming me for that?"

"No! But don't blame me for being just like you."

Danny responded defensively. "I've slowed the drinking way down."

"That's good—for you." Chris was sincere.

Danny took a long look at him before answering. "Yeah. It is." He held his look at his son for a couple of seconds and then said, "Okay, I'm rolling. You want a ride?"

Danny moved off toward the car. After a few beats Chris followed.

CHAPTER 11

THEM THAT DO, THEM THAT DON'T

Anthony was walking down the block to his home at the same time his mother, Carmen, approached from the other direction. For her it was only the end of one part of her daily job, house cleaning. Now she would pick up on her motherly and grandmotherly duties. She had not yet heard the news of Art's death, but Anthony, who heard it that morning, the day after the tragic murder, was about to tell her.

Carmen was in her early fifties, pretty, lean from years of hard work, proud, and strong-willed. She had come to Los Angeles after being smuggled across the border thirty years ago. She was one of those who benefited from the illegal-alien amnesty program, having received legal status with her husband a few years earlier. She had raised two daughters in addition to her youngest, Anthony. Painfully, she knew the hazards that life presented in any given moment only too well, having lost her husband in a car accident when Anthony was five.

Carmen's older daughter, Maria, was working and going to night school. The other daughter, Yolanda, had two children, one an infant, the other a year and a half old. She was in and out of county drug rehab, her current court-ordered home. Though Yolanda was never married, abortion had been out of the question in her mother's Catholic home. Nor was Carmen about to allow adoption. She willingly and gladly provided for her grandchildren, praying every day that her younger daughter would grow worthy of such beautiful children and then take over mothering.

Mother and son met at the four-foot-high chain link gate to their '30s vintage duplex. She looked at her wristwatch and noted the time, 6:45 P.M.

Carmen asked, "Why you come home this late? Officer Art says practice is over at five, hijo."

Anthony was on the verge of crying. "Mama, Art was shot. He's dead."

Carmen immediately made the sign of the cross.

In shock she asked, "Como?"

In barrio s'language, trying to sound tough, he explained that a black gang wanna-be did it, "El Negro quiere estar ganga mayates "

Carmen slapped him. "You don't use those words. You are my son! Mi comprendes? Your proud father's son, bless his soul."

She made the sign of the cross again. Anthony straightened up and quickly responded with a respectful tone. "Si, mama."

Carmen again reprimanded him. "Inglés!"

"Yes, mother."

Then she took her boy in her arms lovingly and guided him up the stairs, into their humble house. Maria, babies in both arms, stepped on the porch as they walked up the front steps. Carmen took the infant from her, kissing him. Anthony took the older baby very lovingly. Carmen's family was safe and together under the roof she worked so hard to keep. Tonight she would pray as always, thankful for the blessing in what they had.

Virginia and John Paul were sitting together over a late dinner. Their little home had a very cozy feeling. It was orderly, something that she required of John Paul and he had learned to respect.

Virginia was a very attractive woman. She had learned the workers' compensation claims business and was making a decent living for her son and herself. Part of her income went to help her family in the Dominican Republic. Were it not for that she and John Paul would have been living in a higher rent area. But Virginia was very loyal to her family. With her son she dealt with an iron fist, usually softened with a velvet glove. She knew it was a tough world and he had to learn to deal with it from her. There was no father around to help.

"Couldn't resist picking up the rifle?" she asked.

"Thought it might be worth something," he responded.

Staring at him, she asked, "Was it worth what happened? Do you get the picture here? If you don't think, you'll get in a lot of trouble."

"I know, I know. I'm sorry."

"No! You don't know." She was trying to hold back her frustration.

"John Paul, I'm not mad. I'm scared. Every day, you go off to school, and I worry. You hang out at the park, playing basketball, and I worry. You could've been the one who was shot. Thank God none of you boys were hurt." She made the sign of the cross.

"Art looked so cold, laying there, mom."

"I'm sorry you saw that, honey." She gave him a long reassuring look, then she hugged him. "Be smart, John Paul. You get shot, there's no second chance. Get in trouble with the law, everything changes."

She moved to the kitchen, coffee cup in hand and added, "I'm proud of you, John Paul."

He sat quietly. She watched for a moment, almost said more, but realized it was better to leave him to his thoughts.

Michael stood alone. Behind him the gate to the basketball court was locked. All that remained of the crime scene was the bloodstained street where Art had fallen and a few chalk marks. Staring at the ground Michael felt a chill he did not understand. The wail of an ambulance siren rolling down Santa Monica Boulevard filled the night with a familiar sound. Michael was standing in the glow of CNN's Hollywood headquarters and a couple of miles below the world's most glamorous sign.

He felt alone and became lost in his thoughts. He wondered if anyone cared about anything besides their own shit.

He began to cry. "I'm sorry, Art. We shoulda gone for Pizza with you. This wouldn't have happened. I'm so sorry." After a few moments he walked off, disappearing into the night.

CHAPTER 12

A FAREWELL IN BLUE

Hundreds of patrol cars, motorcycles, and civilian vehicles were jammed into the Fox Hills cemetery. This last resting site was on a beautiful bluff overlooking the Marina del Rey wetlands and the Pacific Ocean. Most afternoons it was bathed in warm light and ocean breezes. It was the last mortal stop on this earth for the famous and regular people who were simply loved by family and friends.

The Hollywood list was long and included Rita Hayworth, a beauty queen of the silver screen who suffered a tragic end. It also included a major radio star from the '30s, Charles Correll. Charlie had been the voice for the hugely popular radio show character Andy Brown of "Amos n' Andy." Perhaps when the dust settled and the grass had filled in the grave, on some foggy night Charlie and Art would shake hands and have a good spirited discussion about the days in which this white Catholic from Chicago impersonated a black Baptist who moved from Atlanta to Chi town. It could make for a wonderful moment if only we mortals could experience it.

This was a gray day, appropriately overcast. Blue uniforms and city officials were gathered hundreds deep. Art's thirty-seven-year-old wife, Heather, was flanked by Danny and her brother as she sat, feeling alone. She gripped Art's dress cap knowing the finality of the ceremony.

Bagpipes had been playing "Amazing Grace" and now a tenor was delivering those powerful lyrics.

Amazing! How sweet the sound
That saved a wretch like me!
I once was lost, but now am found;
Was blind, but now I see.

T'was grace that taught my heart to fear,
And grace my fears relieved;
How precious did that grace appear
The hour I first believed.

Through many dangers, foils and snares,
I have already come;
'Tis grace hath brought me safe thus far,
and grace will lead me home.

During the singing, Danny helped Heather to Art's flag-draped coffin. With great dignity she placed the cap on it. She took a moment, adjusting the position so the cap sat just the way she imagined Art would have liked. Then she leaned down and kissed the walnut enclosure. She knew this was the final time she would be within inches of her man and so to Heather it was important to say, "I love you, baby."

As she stood up she looked across the interment site at all the people. She saw Mrs. Jones standing with Alonzo, John Paul, Anthony, Michael and Sam. That view brought a thankful smile to her face.

She looked up at Danny and quietly said, "They all loved him. He was right."

Danny nodded, unable to speak. He helped Heather back to her seat as the tenor continued the powerful lyrics.

The Lord has promised good to me...

His word my hope secures.
He will my shield and portion be...
As long as life endures.

CHAPTER 13

THE HOOPS WITHOUT ART

After school the parking lot to the local hamburger stand was alive with cars. Kids poured in and out, escaping the regimen of teachers. This was somewhat an ethnic melting pot: blacks, whites, and Hispanics. And they were driving everything from Mercedes to lowered Chevys. The building and its perimeter fences were painted in vivid colors typical of the Mexican influenced aesthetic. The owner, Mr. Sanchez, allowed local art, the piece-work done by the better taggers. He figured it was better to invite the work than fight it.

Michael and JP, book bags over their shoulders, had cleared the crowd and were moving to the sidewalk.

JP was pushing Michael with his enthusiasm. "We'll keep practicing, that's what!"

A very shapely sixteen-year-old, Roxanne, strutted past them, taking Michael's total attention.

"Yo! Michael," JP said.

Preoccupied, Michael said, "Say you wouldn't hit that."

JP, not that interested, replied, "I wouldn't hit that."

"No, you know."

JP looked at her again, uncomfortably, and said, "Not my style, know what I'm sayin'."

They rounded the corner, and JP picked up the pace.

"Yo, slow your roll," Michael insisted.

"We're late," JP complained.

Michael caught up to him. "You've never done it, have you?"

"What?" said JP, noticeably uneasy.

"Someday you'll get it, dog," Michael said, sounding like the voice of experience.

John Paul whacked him in the arm.

"What about practice? And Art?" JP asked.

"I know, JP. I'm wit it."

"We gotta do something for him," JP added.

"I keep thinkin', if we'd gone with him," Michael mused.

"We've gotta keep the team going. Make moves," JP said with resolve.

They crossed Vine Street and headed for the playground.

John Paul, Michael, Alonzo, Sam, Dennis and Anthony were trying to play ball, but it was chaotic. Older boys interrupted their practice, throwing the boys wise-ass comments.

JP was the organizer. He was going to carry on just as if Art would show up at any moment to intimidate the distracters.

JP took his crew aside.

"Come on, huddle up," he said.

The boys, all frustrated, reluctantly gathered.

"Let's take 'em on. If we do like Art showed us, we can put their sorry asses in the shade," he insisted.

Some jeers came from the sidelines. Michael reacted, zeroed in on one loudmouth and shot him a look. At that moment Crack stepped through the group and quieted the loudmouth. Satisfied, Michael turned back to the huddle.

"I'm gonna set it on him."

"Yeah, yeah. We know you're bad. Talkin' trash, you know what I'm sayin'," remarked Sam.

Alonzo reacted. "Shut up High-top! It's about the game."

Crack approached the boys. "Hey, punks, shoot it or lose it!"

JP looked to the boys for assurance. "What's it? Are we game?"

"No doubt!" Michael asserted.

Dennis shook his head. "Hell no. I'm ghost."

He turned and walked off. Anthony considered following him.

"Punk ass," Michael hissed.

Alonzo leaned on Anthony. "Come on, Tone. We can do it."

Anthony sized things up, looking over his shoulders at the court, the older boys jiving with each other.

"Ese. We can do that," Anthony said, still trying to convince himself.

"A'ight! A'ight!" Sam slapped skins with Anthony.

With a yell of exuberance they broke the huddle.

John Paul turned to Crack. "You wanna play ball?"

Crack smiled. "With you fools?"

"Yeah!" JP's response was in Crack's face.

"Okay, little man. But don't be moanin' when things get rough."

"Stop talkin' shit and play," Michael interjected.

Crack grinned at Michael, but it was threatening. "You a bad ass, boy? Okay, white boy. Show me and my souljas what you got."

JP grabbed Michael and drew him to their end of the court.

Crack's souljas joined him and the scrimmage began.

JP's team played well through their first pattern with a hand-off to JP who sunk a three-pointer. This play was immediately followed with Sam managing to block a shot, then he recovered, passed the ball to Michael, and he took it downtown for another two points.

Michael turned to Crack saying, "My house. You better recognize."

Crack, now pissed, brought the ball in and passed, but the ball bounced off his man's hands, and it dropped out of bounds. Excited, the boys slapped skins. Michael turned to Crack, who held the basketball.

"Man, you a sorry bunch of fools," Michael chided.

"Shut your punk ass mouth," Crack warned.

Crack fired the ball at Michael. Michael brought it in, passed to Sam and the game resumed. It quickly turned into a brawl. Crack, however, did not need to get involved. His boys did it for him.

In the fracas Michael was floored by one of Crack's crew. A tough fighter, Michael was up in an instant, landed a couple of hits, then took some hard hits. It only lasted for a moment, the boys so outsized and outnumbered. Crack's crew chased them off the court.

Sam and Anthony split in one direction while John Paul, Michael and Alonzo walked off toward the center of the playground. They were licking their wounds as they approached the recreation room. A number of adults were entering the building. Three patrol units and a pair of unmarked police cars were parked nearby.

JP was the first to speak. "So much for camp."

Michael was looking back at the basketball court."Who gives a shit?"

"I did," Alonzo replied. He was looking at JP and Michael for an answer. He needed to know. Alonzo lived his life working a little harder than any of his friends because of his weak leg. He never complained. He just did it. And he always believed that he could accomplish anything. The reason: His grandmother told him that every day.

JP looked at Alonzo, but did not know what to say.

Alonzo said it for him. "We'll try again tomorrow."

CHAPTER 14

TAKIN' BACK THE HOOD

The neighborhood had been asked to attend a community meeting with members of the LAPD. This was part of a citywide effort to get the community involved in policing the residential streets. The playground's recreation room provided the logical space for the meeting. Graffiti by neighborhood taggers covered its exterior.

At the folding table dais, Kathy and Danny along with Wilson and three other officers faced a crowd of concerned citizens, who were mostly black and Hispanic with a few whites. JP, Michael, and Alonzo had seen the people entering and they stepped in the room to see what was up.

An older Hispanic man, Emilio Sanchez, was speaking. Though he spoke with broken English, his sincere concern for the neighborhood was evident. No hostility toward the law was evident in his attitude.

"I've got young prostitutes hanging out in front of my business," said Sanchez. His demeanor was that of a very caring person. He added, "This is no good for the others there."

An older black woman added, "And how we gonna get these gangs? You see 'em right out here, hanging round the park, doing their business, mugging folks walking by. You said you was gonna get rid of them."

Many in the audience voiced their agreement. Then an older Latina spoke up. "I point my finger at the gangs, how you going to protect my children? You couldn't even protect your own man."

Danny stood up. "Detective Jackson's death was a mindless act. His killer is in custody. And we're tripling patrols around the park."

Bill Wilson added, "Harass the gangs, just like they've done to you. This is your home."

Danny continued, "We're moving with the D.A's office to invoke a federal law for confiscating property used in drug trade. We'll get the help of property owners. If their renters are selling drugs on the grounds, it's real simple: Evict or lose the property. We'll keep the heat on the gangs till they take it somewhere else."

Sanchez spoke again. "I think I understand. If it's the empty house at the end of my block, I call the owner and insist he does something about it."

Wilson stepped in. "And let us know. We'll up the effort over there."

There was a lot of discussion in the audience. Alonzo's grand-mother, Mrs. Jones, slowly rose. Alonzo saw her and got nervous.

He whispered to JP and Michael, "Let's get outta here."

As the boys quietly left the room, Danny spoke again. "If a rock is thrown through the window of an abandoned house and it's not repaired, it's an invitation to throw more rocks."

Kathy added, "We want to keep repairing the broken windows, so to speak. But we can't do it without your help."

Mrs. Jones spoke up. "The officer's right. We have to get involved."

Sanchez got up, nodding in agreement. "We've got to show the gangs, and the children, that we're takin' back our neighborhood."

Many in the audience voiced their agreement. Sanchez and Kathy exchanged looks. He smiled with appreciation and mouthed the word, "Gracias."

John Paul, Michael, and Alonzo were well up the street at the north-west corner of the playground. Michael noticed some teen girls get-ting out of a school van, dressed for swim practice. He recognized

Alyssum, the girl he bumped into in the subway station.

Michael watched her for a moment from a spot where she would not have seen him. Alyssum and her friends looked out of place in this neighborhood.

JP called out from across the street. "Yo, Michael!"

Michael took another glance at Alyssum, then he jogged across the street and joined his crew. As he approached JP was nodding his head, grinning at him.

"So, who you scheming on?" JP asked cutely.

"The girl from the subway station. You know, I told you about her," Michael answered.

JP looked but could not see any of the girls. He nodded and continued on.

Halfway down the block, the heavy beat of rap boomed from a slow-moving, approaching car. Its passengers were watching the boys. This caught Michael and John Paul's attention. They both saw the rear window of the car go down as one of its passengers pointed a pistol at them.

John Paul and Michael hit the deck. Alonzo, however, was snagging some flowers through a fence and had no clue there was any danger. Michael looked and saw what Alonzo was doing. He reached up and pulled him down hard.

"Yo, what the ?" Alonzo sputtered.

Michael cut him off. "Fool. Shut your face and stay down."

JP added, "Those boyz is foe deep with a Tec 9."

The car continued rolling along, the eyes of the would-be shooter no longer threatening the boys. This time he was satisfied with only scaring boyz in the hood. A few moments ticked off as the car passed harmlessly.

The three boys got to their feet.

Michael began chastising Alonzo. "Locs creapin' up, waving a big-ass gun.

"Yeah, Zo. Pay attention! Or you gonna get fame."

JP noticed the bunch of flowers Alonzo had picked and asked, "Who're those for?"

Timidly, Alonzo said, "Grammy."

Michael was surprised. "Your grandmother? Scoring points, Lonzo?"

Alonzo shook his head. "No. They make her happy. My mom used to bring 'em, before she, you know…"

Alonzo could not say more. He began to tear up as he remembered his mom. She died of an overdose when he was eight. He knew just enough of her to remember the good things.

Michael put his arm around Alonzo, "Yeah, that's all good, bringing Grammy flowers. Just watch your ass, will you, bro?"

John Paul also put his arm around Alonzo. The boys walked on. They were a Dominican, a white, and an African American who saw no color barrier. There was no prejudice among them. They only saw friendship and their love of the game. But they shared another commonality: Not one of these three teens knew their father.

CHAPTER 15

A HOTTIE

Michael led the way, JP and Alonzo right behind him as they entered the parking lot of the hamburger stand. This was the business that Mr. Sanchez ran.

As they passed through a group of teens Michael spotted the hottie, Roxanne, getting in a car.

Michael stopped to watch her, "Oh, yeah, strut your stuff for Michael."

JP noticed. "She ain't doing that for you, fool."

Michael shot back. "You see anybody else around here she's doing that for? Not you, son."

"Son! You sonin' me?" JP asked.

Michael ignored JP and grabbed one of Alonzo's flowers.

Michael turned to JP. "Watch this, and learn."

Alonzo was looking at the few flowers he had left. "Hey, Michael. My flowers."

Michael strutted off like a peacock.

JP could not believe it. "What the...?"

He and Alonzo watched in amazement as Michael put the move on Roxanne. She smiled seductively as he handed her the flowers through the passenger window.

Alonzo was amazed. "Look at that! Did you see that? She took the flower."

JP added, "She took it. She took it!" John Paul was looking on, admiring Michael's confidence.

Michael turned from the car, gliding back to his friends with a grin stretched across his face. The car pulled away as Michael reached the boys.

"What'd you say?" Alonzo asked.

Michael was very cool in his answer. "Some chin music about how she should always have flowers."

Alonzo wanted details. "And what'd she say?"

Michael held up a little piece of paper with a phone number scratched on it. He waved it around, teasing them.

Alonzo asked, "What?"

Michael answered, "She gave me her number, that's what."

JP was loving this but had to challenge him. "You lyin'…"

Michael's smile was totally convincing.

Sanchez was walking across the lot, returning from the community meeting. He started cleaning up the table area in the patio, grabbing a load for the trash can. Michael immediately ran over and began to help him clean tables.

John Paul and Alonzo were dumbfounded. JP said, "What's he up to now?"

Michael made sure Sanchez noticed him as the man returned from the trash area. Michael walked toward him with a trash bundle.

"I'll clean this up for you, Mr. Sanchez."

"Sure, amigo. Gracias."

JP, now totally fascinated, muttered, "Why you sly…"

Michael emptied the trash into the Dumpster. As he returned Sanchez handed him a Coke.

"Thanks." Michael made a big deal out of drinking it.

"You earned it, amigo. Say, you want a regular job?"

"Yeah. That'd be way cool." Michael was pleased. So was Sanchez.

"Good. Come see me tomorrow, after school." Sanchez put out his hand and the two shook.

"Okay, Mr. Sanchez." Michael walked back to JP and Alonzo while Sanchez returned to his kitchen. As Michael joined up with the boys, JP demanded, "No way you did all that for a Coke."

Michael grinned and started toward the sidewalk.

JP added, "Schemer."

At the sidewalk Michael noticed Roxanne standing a little ways down the street. She was talking to Crack and took something from him.

Michael reacted, "What's goin' down, bitch?"

John Paul tugged on Michael to go, but he watched until she got back in the car and left. Crack noticed him watching and laughed before he walked off.

JP hit Michael on the arm to get his attention. The three boys started up the street.

Alonzo asked, "Michael, what was goin' down with Sanchez?"

Michael, still distracted, looked over his shoulder. Then he replied. "Lonzo, I gots me a job. Gonna have me some duckets." And under his breath he added, "To spend on whatever I want."

CHAPTER 16

POPPI

The sun was just setting as Danny, a bag of groceries in hand, stepped onto the porch of a well-kept Craftsman house. It had a nicely manicured front yard, one that had more care than a weekly visit from a gardener. The front porch was flagstone, and it had a comfortable-looking patio rocking chair facing the street.

Danny could see his dad, affectionately known as Poppi, through the kitchen window. Juggling keys and groceries, he managed a wave. Poppi was leaning against the kitchen counter, a cigarette burning in one hand. He was straining to be standing.

Danny turned on a living room light as he closed the door. He passed the large fireplace and then the TV that was on local news. He rounded the corner and walked into the kitchen.

Danny put on a bright face as he headed to the refrigerator, passing Poppi who was taking a seat at the round kitchen table.

"Hey, Poppi. How was your day? Sorry I'm a little late."

Danny was putting away a sixer of Bud, a loaf of white bread, a container of strawberries and a half-pint of cream, all of it under Poppi's watchful eye.

Then Danny handed Poppi a carton of Marlboro Reds. The old man's eyes were bright and clear, but his breathing was labored.

Without missing a beat, Poppi said, "You forgot the eggs."

Danny thought for a second and then realized he screwed up. "Sorry. Musta slipped my mind."

Danny picked up two overfilled ashtrays along with the breakfast dishes and began a nightly routine, straightening up. Poppi watched him without making another comment.

Danny knew his dad only too well and finally asked, "Something wrong?"

Poppi was winded in his response. "You bet something's wrong." He coughed and then continued. "Your boy, my grandson, needs you."

"Dad, if there was a shortcut to growing up, I…"

"If—dog—rabbit." Poppi leaned back.

"What's that supposed to mean?" Danny asked.

"If the dog hadn't stopped to pee he would'a caught the rabbit." Poppi was a wise old country boy.

"Dad, Chris is at a point where he's got to figure life out himself. I can't make him see."

"I didn't have any problem making you see things."

"It was a little simpler then," Danny replied.

"It was damn tough being a parent then, just like it is now. Your mother and I didn't do it by proxy."

Danny took a big breath. He loved his dad and knew everything he said was from a loving heart.

"Dad, all I can do is encourage him. But I'm not living my life for him."

The conversation had hit the wall. Poppi took a moment and lit a cigarette.

"So how's the job?" he finally asked.

Danny was relieved to move off the subject of Chris, one that seemed to have no answer. "Same ol', same ol'."

"Damn proud of you." Poppi was looking at him with his intense blue eyes.

"Thanks, Dad." Danny took a moment and then asked, "How do you feel?"

"With my fingers." Poppi gave no change of expression. He was one hell of a poker player.

Danny sighed, then smiled. "Some night, let's catch a game."

Poppi offered one of his favorite words. "That'd be copasetic, maybe. That is, if these damn legs are up to it."

Danny nodded. After a beat he returned to cleaning. He wondered how much longer his dad's lungs would keep him going. He had been diagnosed with emphysema long before his wife died. To make matters more difficult, Poppi was losing his leg strength from all the years of hard drinking on top of the three packs of smokes he consumed every day. But Poppi was defying the odds as he pushed in on seventy-seven years. He had spent his younger years traveling, first painting electrical towers across the country, then working as a regional salesman, and finally settling down to a local job running a liquor store in the old neighborhood.

It was tough for Poppi to watch his son go through so much pain with Chris, his only grandson. There was something in Chris that reminded Poppi of himself. A fierce independent spirit had kept Poppi from taking the pedestrian track in life, and he could see the same thing in Chris. There was a gene skip, though, and Danny was more the responsible one, never wandering away, always ready to take on whatever was needed.

Poppi admired and loved his boy for all that hard work. But he never had fun with him. Chris was a different story. And Poppi missed him. They had lived together for a couple of years until Danny kicked Chris out. Poppi was still trying to reconcile that day.

CHAPTER 17

L iving in the heart of the old industrial Hollywood was not cool. It was 323. 310 was cool, the area code to the west, starting in Beverly Hills. Anything the teens could do in 310 was taking them to the land of the dukey ropes, fat gold-chain necklaces in hip-hop parlance. That would be gold chains around the neck in their language.

Michael and Sam were heading into the Virgin megastore on Sunset Boulevard, right at the start of the famous Sunset Strip. The Chateau Marmont was across the street about a block west. Hollywood stars had taken refuge within its classic interior for decades, making it a famous haunt. John Belushi spent his last night on this earth in one of its bungalows. From that address west, everything turned to glitter and gold, or so the boys thought.

As Michael and Sam approached the doors of the store, Roxanne and her girlfriend stepped out. The girls were dressed in tank tops with a lot of cleavage, tight pants and a lot of makeup, and those big hoopties, big hoop earrings. Michael turned on the charm as soon as he saw them.

"Roxanne. Yo, whassup?"

Her eyes were dancing. "Michael. Don't tell me. You're rackin' me a CD."

"What you want, homegirl?" he responded.

"You're not a Herb, are you?" she asked.

Sam stepped back. As far as he could see, she was a ho, whore in street terms. And, he could see that Michael was messing with some-one dangerous, someone way beyond him.

Roxanne added, "You gotta have fame, Michael. You got no clout? I can't get down with a sucka. Get some props."

She reached out and seductively kissed her fingertip and then planted it on his lips. With that she rounded the corner out of Michael's view.

Michael looked over to Sam trying to seem confident.

Sam took the liberty of offering his candid thought. "You in trou-ble. Oh yeah. Now you gots a job, you gonna spend all your cash, know what I'm sayin'?"

"High-top, I know what you're sayin'." Michael was defensive, feeling at a loss as to how to manage the Roxanne situation.

"You know what I'm sayin'?" Sam said again.

"Whadaya sayin, High-top?" Michael was annoyed.

"She's a skank. Never be your homegirl. Just another hood rat. That ho cake's thizzin. You a sucka."

Michael became angry and slammed Sam against the wall.

"Bullshit."

Sam easily threw Michael off.

"I hear people talkin' shit, you know what I'm sayin'? I see what I see!" Sam continued, "I ain't dumpin' on the bitch—just sayin' the word."

Michael had no answer. He was caught between his pride, his innocence, and his desire to be a man. Sam had no interest in any con-frontation with his friend and walked off. He read the situation for exactly what it was.

Michael watched Sam for a few moments, then went into the store. As he passed through the security bars he passed Kathy. She was checking out at the cashier's stand and had seen what just went down.

Michael recognized her from the day of the neighborhood meeting in the playground rec room, but had no interest in conversation with a cop. She was no Art Jackson, just a blue-coat Penelope. He passed her without eye contact.

The cashier handed Kathy the CD, "The Red Light District" by hip-hop star Ludacris.

An hour later Kathy and Danny were finishing plates of Cuban-style chicken with onions and fried plantains at Ciudad. It was at the corner of 5th and Figueroa in the shadows of Parker Center, the downtown Los Angeles headquarters of the police department. They were on the patio, sitting below the rising towers of the Bonaventure Hotel and the beautiful downtown skyline. She had a glass of wine and he was drinking a Coke. A Cubano band was setting up across the patio.

"I don't know how you do it," she said.

"What?"

"Raise a kid in this world." She raised her eyebrows as she answered him.

Danny thought a moment. "I hold my breath when the phone rings."

"Even with a son at nineteen?" she asked.

"Now more than ever," he added.

Kathy pondered a thought, then asked, "Ever wonder why you're here?"

"What's to wonder? I just take it a day at a time."

"No, no, what life's all about?" she continued.

The waitress brought the check and Danny grabbed it.

"My treat," he said this keeping the bill out of her hands.

"Thanks," she said, surprised.

"Sixth-graders in gangs, selling cocaine at school. We bring 'em in, twenty-four hours later they're doing the same shit. That's what I wonder about."

"They can't all be like that," she stated.

A moment passed as Danny dealt with his frustration over that entire social area of thought. He wondered if she was too soft at the core or a bleeding-heart.

Finally, he spoke. "You realize this job's not about holding hands. We enforce laws."

Kathy, a strong-minded woman, responded, "Doesn't hurt to help them cross the street. You know, find the path."

Danny came back with, "It's all in the first seven years.

When we get 'em, it's too late."

She did not buy that line of thinking and made it very clear. "That's bullshit, Danny. It's never too late."

Danny studied her face for a moment. "Okay, so this is more than a job for you?"

"I suppose that's true," she answered.

"Good for you," he said sincerely. "In six months I've got twenty years on the job. I think it's great you had the courage to go after this work. Frankly, I can't wait to turn in my badge."

She was cooking on something, working her way up to a comment or thought Danny could tell was important to her. So, out of respect, he gave her a moment.

"Danny, let me tell you about Mrs. Chow, my sixth-grade teacher. I'm talking South Central. Mrs. Chow drove a little blue VW bug. I passed it every day on my way into school. And it had a bumper sticker on the back." Kathy formed the size of the sticker with her hands.

"Bruins. That's what it read. I used to see that sticker and wonder what it meant."

The waitress came by and filled Danny's water glass.

Kathy continued after the waitress walked to the next table, "In those days I had no idea what college was. Going to high school was as far as anyone in my neighborhood even considered. And my folks, they were hard-working people who never had any idea about a black person getting into college or getting out of the neighborhood."

Danny was listening, paying close attention. She was speaking from her heart, and he recognized it.

Kathy continued, "One day after class I asked Mrs. Chow what the sticker on her car meant. 'Bruins? Why that's the mascot for the university I went to, Anita,' she said. 'That's a school you should go to,' she added. And I asked what kind of school it was. 'UCLA. It's a university. You could go there after you go to high school. If you do that, Anita, you'll be able to do anything you want with your life.' Danny, Mrs. Chow is the reason I went to college. It happened to me right there. Sixth grade. What was I? Eleven maybe. So don't tell me by seven it's too late. It's never too late."

She had really nailed him. He suddenly felt like a complete bigot, showing all the prejudice that he never wanted to experience, let alone put forth.

After a moment he spoke. "That's a wonderful story, really wonderful. You honored your parents in telling it to me and paid tribute to someone who changed your life. I'm sorry I said what I did before. It came out with the wrong inflection. I know there's a lot of kids out there that need a break in life. But there's also a lot of them who are either long past salvation or would never understand our way of life. Their beginnings and only life references have kept them in the dark."

Kathy knew enough from her own childhood, attitudes of neighbors and the ways of that part of the city. Danny certainly had his point. She also knew it was time to go home.

At that moment the band started its first set. They were hot and tight with brass, sax, guitar, bass, piano, drums, timbales, and two singers.

"Thanks for dinner," she offered.

Danny grunted something about charging the department as he started for the register.

Then she remembered the CD in her pocket and handed it to him at the register. He had begun moving to the infectious Cubano music.

He looked at the cover. "Ludacris?"

"Yeah. You ought to listen, learn something."

He reached into a bowl of chocolate mints, counted a handful to himself then handed the cashier two bills. He offered Kathy a mint, still dancing.

"Want one?"

"Can you spare it?" she quipped.

He looked down at his hand, overflowing with mints.

Cutely he said, "I don't know. What do you think?"

She took one.

Then he coyly said, "That'll cost you one dance."

This caught Kathy totally off-guard. Before she could say no, he dumped the candies in his pocket, took her hand, and led her in a cha-cha on the edge of the patio, just outside the front entrance to the restaurant.

She said, "I don't know how to do this."

He smiled and said, "Looks good. Just follow me."

She did, and they had a lot of fun. This was a moment of departure for both these hard-working people. Kathy was watching him move. He was lost in the music. She let it take her over as well.

After the second song he started for the stairs, but he kept the dancing going as he moved along. Passers-by could not help but watch them and smile.

As they crossed the footbridge over Figueroa he offered her another mint. They were now above the patio, and the music still filled the night.

She took it and with a sly grin said, "Guess I'll owe you another dance."

He nodded his approval. Then he stopped his dancing and said, "On another night." He smiled.

"We should paint it," she said.

"What?" he asked.

"The graffiti on the rec room. Let's organize a paint detail. We'll get help from the neighbors."

Danny dug out his keys from his pocket as he walked and with a grin said, "Great idea. You organize it. Let me know how it turns out."

She smiled back and said, "I will." Then she winked.

Across the street their cars were parked in a temporary zone at the hotel. The security man waved to Danny as they walked up.

At her car, she said, "Good night, Danny." She still wore the grin.

Danny looked back at her, wondering what her wily grin was about. He was soon to discover that when Kathy Montalvo put her mind to something, she would move heaven and earth to accomplish her goal.

CHAPTER 18

A paint roller took a diagonal swipe, leaving a fresh path of beige paint that covered the black spray-painted graffiti.

It was a Saturday morning, and Kathy and Danny were painting the community center recreation room. She was still wearing her wily grin. He was grumbling under his breath with each roller swipe.

Danny stopped and looked over to her. "I can't believe this. You know I'm giving up my Saturday morning breakfast at Sal's."

She kept on painting, ignoring his complaining.

Danny continued, "That's like religion for me."

"This will give you a new kind of faith, trust me," she responded.

A pair of twelve-year-old boys rode up on their bikes to watch. They were the first of the neighborhood who came over to investigate. Others across the street were speculating, though. Danny was in a grumpy mood and made a face at one of the boys. The boy shot a look back at him that made Danny smile.

The other boy asked, "Say, mister, why you doin' that?"

Danny replied, "My friend here likes to paint. Want to learn how? It's loads of fun.

"No thanks." His friend shook his head signaling a flat no-way. As the boys made ready to roll, Kathy turned to Danny.

"Oh, you're good." Then she called out to the boys, "Hey, guys, want some of these?"

They stopped and looked. Kathy pulled trading cards from her pocket and waved them. Eagerly, they each took a couple. Just behind them Grandmother Jones walked toward the rec room with Alonzo and John Paul reluctantly in tow.

Kathy, seeing that the bikers were now quite happy, gave them the price of her kindness. "So, you guys want to give us a little help?"

The leader was suddenly quite agreeable saying, "Sure."

Danny cutely commented, "Bribery's not fair."

Kathy noticed Mrs. Jones and the two boys approaching, so she called out, "Hi, there."

Mrs. Jones responded with a big smile. "Hello."

The woman was out of breath as she admired the paintwork. Alonzo and JP, were awkward, embarrassed, and definitely under the command of this iron-willed grandmother.

"I'm Francis Jones. I was here, at the meeting."

"Yes." Kathy turned to JP and Alonzo. "Hey, guys. How's it going?"

They mumbled hellos.

"Well, you really are painting." Mrs. Jones sounded amazed, and at the same time, seemed proud.

Danny, showing off the paint dribbles on his hands and shirt, said, "Word spreads fast, kinda like the paint, ma'am."

Kathy asked, "Mrs. Jones, you're surprised?"

Mrs. Jones responded, "Very pleased. And my grandson, Alonzo, and his friend John Paul, are volunteering, since it's Saturday."

Danny was quite pleased at the news. "Well, isn't that nice."

The boys forced smiles.

Mrs. Jones turned to the boys. "Good. Now I'm leaving. And don't wipe your hands on your clothes."

"Yes, Grandma," said Alonzo.

Danny piped in, "Yes, ma'am. I promise you that."

She turned to him, smiling, knowing he was teasing. "Good boy." Then she chuckled to herself and added, "You're a character, aren't you, detective?"

Danny winked.

Kathy added, "Thanks, Mrs. Jones."

Mrs. Jones responded, "No. Thank you. This is terrific. Anyway, the boys have nothing more important to do."

Alonzo wasn't accepting that comment. "Grandma! Basketball?"

Mrs. Jones replied. "What did you tell me? You wished you could of helped Art. Well?"

The boys nodded agreement.

Mrs. Jones, now a few steps away turned back and said, "Be home by six."

And with that she was gone.

Under his breath Alonzo could only say, "Sorry, Art."

Kathy turned to Danny and asked, "What do you think would happen if there were more Grandmother Joneses around here?"

Danny chuckled to himself. "We'd probably be out of a job."

He took a moment and then said to his captives, "So, boys, let me demonstrate."

The boys joined in and started rolling paint on the building. They got the hang of it immediately and seemed to enjoy the improvement of the building. Alonzo asked Danny, "You knew Art?"

Danny responded. "He was my best friend, Alonzo. You and me doing this together would make him real happy."

Alonzo went back to the painting, comforted by the thought.

For both boys, Art was very present in their minds. Being on the playground almost brought him back.

•

As the day progressed they all worked a little, played a little, teased each other and enjoyed the experience. During it all Sam and Anthony happened by with a basketball, only to get drawn into the painting. And for good measure, a few neighborhood folks came over to help. During it all Danny was pleased to have an LAPD patrol unit give them a squawk as it cruised the neighborhood. By mid-afternoon the rec room had a fresh coat of paint. The group stood back and admired the work, taking pleasure in the fact that they had taken back something for themselves and the neighborhood. The work finished, the neighbors drifted on with their business.

Just as the boys were about to split, Kathy picked up Sam's basketball and did a quick spin on her index finger followed by a couple of quick moves that got immediate attention from Danny and the boys.

Danny asked, "What was that?"

"A little pent-up energy," Kathy responded. Then she threw a hard, fast pass to John Paul.

He was surprised with the strength of the pass.

Kathy asked, "Officer Smith and I would love to shoot some hoops, if you're up for the challenge?"

With raised eyebrows Danny said, "I've got things to do."

Kathy quickly responded, "So did they. Come on. I'll spot you a few points."

Danny puffed up. "I don't need you spottin' me points."

The boys were up for this experience. Feeling a testosterone rush of male dominance, they could not wait to see if she could really shoot.

•

Kathy was a real competitor and clearly enjoyed playing with Danny and the boys. Surprised would not come close to describing the male reaction to this female, who, with absolute command of the game, ran circles around them.

Michael showed up shortly after they began playing, and watched from the sidelines in disbelief. The woman clearly outplayed the boys. The scene drew the attention of others as Crack and his friends passed by. They watched, also amazed but at the same time resentful of her presence.

Having humbled the men enough to prove her skill, Kathy backed off and encouraged the boys to play against each other. John Paul went up against Sam. Frustration with the tall defender got the better of JP as Sam used his height to block several of John Paul's shots.

Kathy figured it was a good time for the boys to take a break; she did not want trouble developing between them.

She took the ball after a missed rebound and said, "Hey, let's take five."

Danny, a little winded and glad to rest, still managed to be playful saying, "Too much for you, I know."

Kathy nodded sarcastically. She noticed JP walking toward the shady spot where Michael was sitting and went to join them. Danny and Anthony walked to the drinking fountain, leaving Sam on the court shooting hoops. He was just getting warmed up and did not want to break his rhythm.

Anthony was still amazed at how Kathy played. "Chinga tu madre. That chick is good," he said to Danny.

"Ran my legs off. Wonder where she learned to play like that." Danny was still amazed and shook his head in disbelief.

By this time, Kathy had joined Michael and JP. "Hey, name's Kathy."

Michael was not much interested in Kathy. As she spoke to him he looked off toward Crack and his gang friends moving across the park.

She continued, "You play?"

Michael forced out a reply. "Yeah."

"Any good?" she inquired.

"Good enough," he said cockily, not looking at her.

Kathy turned her attention to JP. "So, John Paul, you can get past Sam."

JP snapped. "How? He's all over me."

"Send him in the wrong direction with a hard body fake," she said casually. "Sell it with your shoulders. He'll be off-balance. You're quick. Won't matter how tall he is."

JP thought about what she said.

Sam was getting impatient and looked over from the court. "You punks gonna get your sorry asses back out here? You know what I'm sayin'."

JP got up and walked on the court.

Michael finally looked at Kathy. "How you know that? Girls don't know that shit."

"Michael, when you spend everyday after school on courts like these, fighting for your place against all the boys, you learn." Saying that revived distant memories of her days on the playground courts, just like this one.

Kathy snapped back to the moment and asked, "Why don't you play? I'll watch."

Michael nodded and took to the court.

"Yo, JP," he called out as he moved across the court.

John Paul turned to him as he asked, "Why you playing with that Penelope?"

"She's helping. So what she's a cop. You got a problem?" JP looked straight in his eyes for an answer.

Michael was surprised by JP's directness. "I ain't got a problem."

"Then let's play," Michael said.

Danny tossed the ball to JP. "Okay, you guys bring it on."

Michael showed his stuff as the play resumed, wanting to impress Kathy. She watched John Paul though, knowing he was someone who wanted to learn, and she could reach him.

JP tried Kathy's suggestion and to his pleasure, it worked. He did the hard body fake and went in for a layup.

After a round of high-fives John Paul could not resist looking over at Kathy. She gave him an enthusiastic thumbs-up.

But in the next moment, joy turned into the pain of the streets as a woman's scream washed over them like a tidal wave.

Heads turned to see what was happening.

One hundred yards away, across the field and on the sidewalk, a woman was struggling to keep her purse from a seventeen-year-old boy.

Danny broke into a dead run toward the scene, with Kathy on his heels. John Paul, Michael and Alonzo followed while the others watched from a distance.

As Danny and Kathy got closer, the robber threatened the woman with a knife. She was determined not to give it up, and continued to fight to keep her purse from the teen. Seeing the approaching threat of Danny and Kathy, the teen finally took a savage slash at the purse strap, cutting it and gashing the woman's arm. In shock she let go of the purse. The attacker ran with the purse clutched in his hands as Danny and Kathy closed within twenty yards.

A few people moved closer now that Danny and Kathy were arriving. The injured woman was holding her badly cut arm.

Danny turned to the crowd and called out, "Someone call 911! Request an ambulance!"

Danny turned his attention to the victim. She was going into shock and lost her legs, dropping to the sidewalk. Michael, John Paul and Alonzo were now close enough to see what Danny was dealing with.

Kathy was keeping her eye on the robber. As he ran, he was so distracted looking over his shoulder to see how close his pursuer was, he fell.

"I'm after him!" she yelled, sprinting in pursuit.

Danny looked up from the victim to see what Kathy was doing. "Shit!"

"I'll call for the ambulance," a woman in the crowd offered.

Danny was fixated on Kathy. He yelled to her, "Don't do that! Wait for backup!" With that Danny was on the chase too.

An alley paralleled the street Kathy was on. Danny hesitated as he sized up the situation. He took the alley. In the background the boys were following, their adrenaline pumping. They crossed the street to follow Kathy.

A block and a half from the playground, the robber ran up to Crack who was standing by a customized '62 Chevy. A driver was ready behind the wheel with the motor running. The robber tossed the purse to Crack, who tossed it to the driver.

Crack saw that Kathy was coming. He motioned with his eyes to the robber, who immediately got in the car.

He simply said, "Roll!"

As the Chevy pulled away Crack looked toward Kathy who had slowed her approach. She was two car lengths away, and confidently walked within one car length of Crack.

He asked her, "You lost?"

Kathy said nothing and continued toward him.

Crack added, "No basketball court here."

"Your friend committed a felony," Kathy said, matter-of-factly.

"What friend?" He was looking around, palms open.

"The one in that car," she said, gesturing after the Chevy.

"Oh? I don't see no car," he responded innocently.

Danny was cautiously approaching behind Crack, parked cars his cover.

"You helped him get away. Makes you an accessory. So, I think we need to go downtown," Kathy said.

"Who the hell are you? Movin' like you da man!" Crack said with disdain.

Kathy pulled her badge from her hip pocket, flashed it, and replaced it while saying, "I am the man. And you're going downtown."

Crack took a step toward her with major attitude. "You the one goin' down, bitch."

Kathy drew her service revolver from under her shirt and aimed it at his upper torso. Her eyes went from the woman with a concern for kids to someone primal in that instant.

"Hands behind your head, slowly. Interlock your fingers," Kathy commanded.

Crack responded slowly.

"On your knees," she continued.

As he lowered himself to his knees, she pulled back the hammer on the pistol, cocking it. The trigger was a hair away from releasing the fury of a 9mm bullet. "Sneeze and they'll scrape your head off the sidewalk," Kathy warned.

Kathy had seen Danny moving in from behind Crack. He smoothly took Crack's left hand and hooked him up with cuffs.

Without taking his eyes off Crack, Danny eased Kathy back. "I got him, Montalvo."

With Crack's hands secured behind his back, Danny raised him to his feet. Kathy kept the weapon pointed at Crack.

"Montalvo." Danny's voice was stern.

Kathy slowly lowered her weapon, reset the hammer and holstered it as a pair of units rolled to the curb.

Wilson and Tyler were out of the first car and two patrolmen got out of the second. Still standing behind Crack, Danny patted him down. He found a pistol under his shirt.

Danny handed Crack over to Tyler saying, "Book him—concealed weapon."

Tyler placed Crack in the back of his unit as Danny handed the weapon to Wilson.

Wilson took the weapon and commented, "He'll probably make bail in two hours."

Danny responded as positively as he could. "So it's a cleaner street 'til he's out."

Kathy asked, "What about the mugger?"

Danny asked, "You get the plates?"

She struggled trying to remember. "Sam, Bravo—I'm not sure. I think it was a '62 Chevrolet."

Danny took over. "The mugger was five ten, black. Maybe eighteen. Carrying a knife. Consider him dangerous. You know the drill." Then he turned to Kathy. "Come on."

The two basketball players, suddenly-turned-cops, passed through the crowd in front of Michael, John Paul and Alonzo. In that moment all three of them realized something they had not connected with. These people who were teaching them basketball were real police officers. They have to enforce the laws of the land. Sometimes that meant force. This was no video game. This was no episode of "The Shield." This was real, and it happened in front of them. They had seen the victim's blood-soaked arm. They saw the gun come out from under Crack's shirt.

As the crowd dispersed, the boys headed back toward the courts.

Danny and Kathy were around the corner. Danny was walking at a pretty good clip, making her work at staying up with him. He stopped and turned to her, first making sure no one was watching.

"You damn fool."

Kathy was suddenly indignant. "Me?"

"You're lucky you aren't dead. If that asshole thought he could get away with it, he would have popped you on the street. Don't do it again."

"What? Be a cop?" she replied. "We graduated from the same academy!"

"And they trained you to wait for your partner. Or did you miss that lesson?" Even though his sarcasm came through, he was only concerned about safety, and the following of proven procedure.

Kathy, on the other hand, was prideful. "If I were a guy, this conversation would never have happened."

Danny responded, "Oh, please. Don't lay that feminist crap on me. You're smarter than that." His frustration with her had gotten the better of him. He began to settle down and changed his tone to concern. "Just let me know what you're thinking before you jump in." Then he disarmed her when he added, "Okay, partner?"

Kathy's defensive posture dropped away and she acknowledged her emotional reaction. "I saw that woman, her arm bleeding, that scum running." But then she admitted, "Okay, I know you're right. I should'a checked first."

He nodded slowly and then smiled. They continued walking.

"Say, you're some kind of ballplayer, man! Oops—woman."

She slammed him in the shoulder. He feigned pain, then laughed. "Where'd you learn to shoot?"

"UCLA. NCAA champions. In fact, I was the high point scorer in the championship game my senior year," giving him a power-fist gesture.

Danny shook his head in amazement. Then he cutely asked, "No shit. You've had your legs shortened?"

"Very funny."

"Well, you can't blame me. Who would ever guess you're a basketball star." he added.

She proudly added, "Hall of Famer."

"Wow. No wonder you kicked my ass." Teasing her he went further. "You know, that's really unfair. You were taking advantage of me, in my innocence."

"Please. Innocent you are not." She was comfortable with the banter. She'd learned a long time ago how to deal with sport jocks.

They crossed the street, heading back to the park and the courts. Kathy started to say something, stopped herself, then blurted it out.

"Let's coach the boys. Pick it up where Art left off."

Her words stopped Danny. "It's one thing to go to a meeting, or spend an afternoon painting. It's another to hang your pretty butt on that court every day."

Kathy smiled. "With you beside me, hey, what more could a girl need?"

Danny rolled his eyes. "Why am I even bothering to say this?"

He moved on.

She added, "You know, if they're good enough I was thinking we'd get 'em into a basketball competition. You know, the Southern Cal summer sports competition for kids. They'll come from all over L.A. County."

Danny cocked his head. "You are crazy."

She ignored him. "I was thinking about entering them in the PAL statewide competition too, next February.

He couldn't believe his ears. "That is serious stuff. You talking about the state Police Activities League games?"

Kathy answered, "Next winter. This summer it's the So Cal competition."

"Hell, they'll need uniforms, a place to stay for the week, not to mention being a team."

"They can be ready if they want it enough," she replied.

"It's not the kind of police work I'm normally doing, you know. And it takes a lot of time," he added.

She nodded her head in agreement. "I suppose it will."

Danny looked down for a moment. He was trying to find some reason to say no. He looked to the sky as if he was about to ask the heavens for help. Then he looked at her firmly, with his best tough-guy look and said, "At camp, I won't cook for them."

Kathy burst out laughing. It was as much relief as it was joy that he had agreed to join in with her.

She gave him a high-five and he returned it. And then they continued to the playground. On the way Danny remembered conversations with Art, how much coaching those boys did for his soul. Inside Danny knew that he would step in for Art. But now with Kathy, he was going to do something with a pro. He imagined how happy Art would have been to have Kathy joining up with him. And then Danny thought about Chris. Somehow, maybe working with these boys would give him some insight to communication with his own boy.

CHAPTER 19

Michael rounded the corner and came up on Alyssum, who was waiting curbside alone. Her hair was wet, and she was dressed in hip athletic clothing. She saw him and flashed a natural smile.

Michael was intimidated by her unvarnished quality. She had such bright, inquisitive eyes that he was unable to hold a concentrated look at her without having his eyes dart elsewhere. Her sincerity was evident, but to Michael, something about her naïve openness was disarming. Having trouble understanding what he was feeling, he smiled slightly and said, "Hey."

Cutely she responded, "Hay? That's what horses eat!"

Michael was a little red in the face. "Huh?"

She read his reaction and felt compelled to explain her joke. "My riding coach always says that. Funny when I'm at the stable, but kinda dumb here, I guess," she said.

"You, own a horse?" he asked in amazement. The thought was beyond his comprehension.

"An Arabian. His name is Amir." Michael could see her eyes sparkle as she spoke about her horse. "The name's sooo him." Michael asked, "What's it mean?"

"Commander. He's such the boss."

Michael was really impressed. "That's so cool."

"Yeah." She was nodding her head, getting more animated by the moment. The unexpected encounter was making her nervous, but Michael could not have known: He was so self-conscious.

Michael looked around realizing that she was alone and knew she did not fit the neighborhood. "So, what are you doin' around here?"

"My school's redoing their pool so we're practicing here for a while."

A moment of awkward quiet and Michael almost moved off.

Alyssum picked up the conversation. "I'm on the swim team."

He nodded but had no idea what to say next.

She quickly asked, "So what're you doin' here?"

"Basketball practice."

Brightly, she offered, "I like basketball."

"The hoops. It's the game."

She said suddenly, "My name's Alyssum."

"I'm Michael."

"Hi, Michael."

"I'm still embarrassed about knocking your stuff over in the subway station." He realized as he said those words that he suddenly felt comfortable talking to her. He added, "Did you say Melissum?"

She twisted her nose, "I know it's hard to get. My mother gave me this name. No one has it. Alyssum. It's a flower. I'm sorry."

"What are you sorry for? It's way cool that no one's got your name. I mean, how many Michaels are there?"

She chuckled nervously and asked, "How often do you practice?"

"My crew picks up games. It's different now. We used to practice with Art. He was coaching us till the…" He did not want to say the words.

She put his words together with the news she had heard and finished his thought. "Was he the policeman that…"

"Yes."

"I'm so sorry." Her eyes showed him she meant it.

A new Mercedes sedan pulled up with Alyssum's mother driving. The car said power and wealth and was intimidating for Michael. Janice, late thirties, was attractive and well-kept.

"See ya, Alyssum," he said as he started on his way.

"You said it perfect." Then with hopefulness, she added, "See you next time I practice—okay?"

Michael could not believe that this pretty girl, coming from her part of town, would have any interest in him. Sarcastically he replied, "Yeah, right." Then to himself he muttered, "Like you really need to hang out with a loser."

Alyssum did not hear either of his comments. She watched him for a moment and then got in the car.

"Hi, honey," her mom said while leaning in to kiss her on the cheek.

"Hi."

The Mercedes rolled down the block.

"How was practice?" her mother asked.

"Good."

Quietly, they rode on. Finally her mother asked the burning question, "Who was that you were talking to?"

"A boy."

"I could see that."

Alyssum looked at her. "He plays basketball at the playground. Just someone I met, Mom."

Janice took the interrogation no further but knew instinctively, the boy was someone special to her daughter.

Michael had stopped at the corner to watch the Mercedes take Alyssum away. He wondered what her life must be like, this pretty innocent-looking girl.

CHAPTER 20

It was late afternoon when Danny and Kathy stepped on the court interrupting JP, Michael, Anthony, and Sam in their half-court game. Alonzo was taking shots from the top of the key at the other end of the court. He was practicing what was a difficult shot for any young man, but especially difficult for Lonzo because of the weakness in his left leg.

Danny walked directly to Michael. "Hey, my man. How you doing?"

"I ain't your man." Michael turned away.

Kathy slapped the ball out of Sam's hands, turned toward JP and said, "Hey, guys. How are you?" She gave JP a handgrip that told him she knew the street.

JP returned it. Alonzo followed, as did Sam and Tone. Michael was another story. He hung back.

Danny was anxious and just blurted out, "Look, it's like this. We thought you might keep the team happening."

Kathy added, "You worked hard with Art. Let's keep it going."

The boys exchanged looks of surprise. Michael, however, was not willing to show any interest. To him, these two adults seemed an intrusion on the courts. JP sensed that Michael was going to make some negative comment and shot Michael a look that kept him silent.

JP stepped up and spoke. "We were gonna ask you."

Kathy smiled. "Now you don't have to."

Danny put out his hand in a hold motion. "Okay, great. So, where did Art leave off?"

"He was gettin' us used to passing," JP said.

Alonzo filled in, "Setting up the shot."

Danny asked, "So, how you doing with the move?"

Michael piped up, "Just gimme the ball, I'll make the moves."

Sam turned to him. "Shut up, Michael. You know what I'm sayin'?"

Danny interrupted. "Wait a sec. Easy. What did you learn from Art?"

Sam spoke first. "There's more to the game than taking a shot. You know what I'm sayin'."

Kathy nodded.

JP added,"That no one's more important than the other." Anthony jumped in. "That we aren't five but really one."

Danny liked hearing that. "Right, one team. Thank you, Art."

Kathy passed the ball to JP. "But there's a condition for Danny and me being here."

The boys waited to hear. She pointed to the rec room and said, "The graffiti on the rec room."

They looked at the freshly tagged walls.

She continued, "You help us keep those walls painted, and we'll help you."

Michael asked, "Why bother?"

Kathy turned to him. "Call it an exchange. We help you, you help the neighborhood."

It took only a moment for the boys to quickly agree.

JP, feeling like the spokesman for the crew, stepped up and said, "Okay."

Kathy nodded and looked over to Danny, who nodded back.

"Okay, let's play," Danny said and clapped his hands.

And the practice began.

That afternoon Danny worked with Sam and Anthony while Michael, John Paul and Alonzo worked with Kathy. They had the boys practice every move imaginable from running patterns back and forth, dribbling, guarding drives, doing sidestep exercises, everything except taking a shot.

During the grueling session, Roxanne and a girlfriend walked by and watched from the shade of a tree. The boys noticed the girls, especially Michael. He wanted to show his stuff, but the practice drill did not give him the opportunity.

JP finally asked, "Why don't we run some plays?

Michael added, "Yeah, I wanna shoot."

The others mumbled agreement.

Kathy was uninterested. "If you want more, you gotta pay more. Work for it, you know what I'm saying?"

The boys said nothing.

Kathy asked, "Are we wasting my time here?"

JP began the practice exercise again and the others followed his lead, except Michael. His frustration was getting the better of him as he saw Roxanne and her friend walking away. He grabbed a ball, ignoring Danny, and took a shot just outside the key, sinking a three-pointer. He walked away immediately, his finger gesturing straight down, the symbol for having made his shot clean.

Michael called out loudly enough for everyone to hear. "I came here to shoot hoops. Ain't got time for that shit."

John Paul was pissed and started after him, but Danny fired the ball to him. "Forget him. Keep your head in the game."

As practice restarted, John Paul made eye contact with Michael. It was a hard look between friends, and it carried a lot of resentment. Kathy saw this and called JP out.

Just off the court she got his attention. "John Paul, you want to get emotional, you want to be pissed off at your friend— bring all that mental baggage on the court and into the game, then don't waste your teammates' efforts. 'Cause if you do that, you're going to lose, not just you—but the team."

He was looking at her, listening to every word. What she was saying he understood. He nodded.

"So, what's it going to be?" she asked.

"I want to play, coach."

"Okay. Then get back in there."

As JP returned to the court, Kathy lingered. Across the playground she could see Michael walking away. She was not ready to give up on him. But for the time being, Kathy Montalvo had her hands full with JP, Alonzo, Sam, and Anthony.

How could she have known, in what now seemed a lifetime ago when she was a sophomore at Los Angeles High School that she was in training for her eventual adult role as a mentor to at-risk teenage boys?

Through her experience Kathy had become a strong advocate of the pursuit of education. She understood that her years at UCLA polished the edges and gave her an inner strength. The power she felt was a product of both the confidence she gained and the academic subjects she had learned. The statement on the paper credential served to convince Kathy that she could enter the game of life at a level well beyond her youthful expectations. However, Kathy often reflected on what she did not learn in any classroom.

In her high school days, organized girls' basketball was embryonic. Her senior year, only four games for the varsity girls' team were scheduled compared to twelve for the boys' varsity squad. Kathy loved the game and knew she needed time on the courts. Her option was singular: It meant hanging out at the public courts on Pico Boulevard.

Those playgrounds were not much different today. Drive past any of them and you'll see boys and men playing pickup ball. You will rarely see a woman in their midst. Had you been driving down Pico in Kathy's high school days, odds are you would have seen a five-seven pretty, dark-skinned girl fighting for her place on the courts amid a group of tough male competitors who did not want a girl sharing court space.

There's no room to be a "girl" in that circumstance. Kathy was swimming with the sharks. She learned right there the meaning of the saying, "it's a dog eat dog world." On the public courts there was no official in black-and-white stripes, no referee, no teacher to call a tough kid out and send him to the principal's office. It was every man for himself. And if you were a lonely girl, it was every man against one girl—who was very alone.

Survival of the fittest, the laws of the jungle, means essentially— do what you need to endure. That was and still is the recipe for the amount of stamina it takes. Drop one inch, be a slacker, suggest something was not fair, you're toast. You might as well go home and have milk and cookies.

Kathy remembered those days, fighting for a place on the court. She'd been slammed to the ground more times than she could remember. She knew that earning respect came from the willingness to do whatever it takes. Kathy rose to the call. She had a natural instinct for the game. She also had a God-given talent and was one fantastic shooter. But on those nose-bleed afternoons, she learned how to outlive an opponent. Some call that street smarts or the school of hard-knocks.

When Kathy started playing basketball at UCLA, she had been schooled on the public courts. There was never a set of eyes she looked into on the court that took her confidence. Had she only played organized sports as a teen, in the protected environment of the school grounds, who knows how good she would have been in the eyes of the NCAA.

But for now Kathy was looking at Michael. There was a boy with a lot of natural talent and an opportunity to survive the test in life he now faced. Kathy wanted to help him find his way past the neighborhood. Would he allow her?

CHAPTER 21

COME TO MY OFFICE

Michael was halfway across the field. His best friends were doing some weird practice that had nothing to do with the game, as he saw it. He wanted to be on the court with them, but he wanted to shoot, make those inside moves he loved so much. The falling of a three-pointer, or driving in from the top of the key and making that layup—this was the game. He looked back and saw his crew still doing those stupid exercises. He caught Kathy's eyes for a moment but looked away.

Roxanne was talking to some friends, and Michael decided to casually move in her direction. Before he got to her, Crack stepped out of the shade of a tree where his souljas were hanging. He approached Michael.

"Hey, my man."

"I ain't your man," Michael snapped.

"Easy, son." Crack gave him some skin. They slapped and Crack commented, "Yeah. Everything's cool."

Michael was not sure what to make of this sudden friendliness.

"Still pissed 'cause you got your ass kicked by my crew?" Crack asked with a wicked smile.

"My team was beating you. You know it." Michael was not about to let this slick, hip-hop gangsta, think he got the better of him.

"Yeah. You're cool. I watch you shootin' hoops. You're good. You're good," Crack said, nodding. He was sizing Michael up, head to toe.

"Come to my office," Crack added, gesturing to his friends a few yards away. Michael walked with him, cautiously.

Crack continued, "I gots me a gig. Plenty of duckets. You want in?"

Michael replied, "I gotta job."

Crack almost laughed. "Working for Sanchez?"

"Yeah!" said Michael. He was proud of his job.

Crack took out a wad of bills and thumbed the roll.

"Yeah. You got a job."

The meeting was making Michael uncomfortable. He glanced over his shoulder to the courts, then back to Crack.

"I seen them arrest you," Michael blurted out.

Crack's expression changed as his eyes turned cold, like a predator's.

Crack put the roll back into his pocket. "Go back to your pig friends, fool."

Crack walked off. Michael watched him for a moment, then looked back at the courts. His buddies were deep in their practice. Then he looked at Roxanne.

Crack approached his crew, still hot over Michael's comment about Crack's arrest.

One of his souljas asked, "Why you messin' with whitey?"

Crack snapped back, "That whitey is my ticket to be doin' biz with his white homies. You get that, fool?"

The teen backed off. Crack turned and looked back at Michael, who was walking up to Roxanne.

Crack watched Michael approaching Roxanne, one of his favorite customers, and added, "A little time with that ho—that boy'll be doin' whatever I tell him."

Crack turned back to his crew. "Now, get outta my face."

His boyz scattered, leaving him his space.

Roxanne saw Michael approaching and moved away from her friends to speak with him.

"Michael," she said with a seductive head turn, "whassup?"

"Nothin'. Where you goin'?"

She reached out and touched his chest. "You a—player?"

Michael looked back toward the courts and then answered, "I shoot good."

She was amused by his naiveté and he was immediately embarrassed.

"What?" he asked.

"Wanna know what I tried last night, Mikey?"

He just stared, afraid to guess.

She mouthed the words with her heavily painted lips.

"E-C-S-T-A-S-Y. My body, it was all tingly. I took off all my clothes, and I slipped into the water. I imagined I was the water and you were inside me. You hard yet?"

Michael looked around to see if anyone was watching.

"What you talkin' that shit for?" he asked. "Sure, I wanna be with you."

Roxanne gestured to Crack. "Score some Eee from your friend—I'll meet you at Liquid. Tonight. I need S-E-X! Can you run a train?"

With that, she turned on her heels and walked back to her friends. Michael was stunned. What had she just suggested? If he brought Ecstasy with him to a club, would they have sex? His mind was racing with a variety of arousing images. But that would mean doing business with Crack. He was getting paid by Sanchez later, but would need all of the money to cover being at a club with Roxanne.

Normally he would have talked this kind of thing over with JP. They checked everything out together. But that wasn't going to happen now. Michael looked over to the courts feeling removed from his friends.

As he turned to leave, he noticed Alyssum and her swim team at the pool. They were getting ready for a practice. She and one of her friends were talking. To Michael it appeared the friend was watching him. He thought she probably saw him talking to Roxanne. The sight of Roxanne would definitely tell Alyssum that Michael was not her type. But then Michael did not believe he had a chance with Alyssum anyway, so what difference could it make?

Michael walked off. Behind him was everything important in his life: friends, the game, the girl.

CHAPTER 22

BRINGING HOME THE LAUNDRY

Kathy made her way down the corridor of the second floor of the Hollywood police station. It was another day on a job that had no end. There was a rhythm being on the street, something that Kathy preferred. Office work, by definition, is confining. For an athlete, the air inside is stale.

Detective Tyler stepped from the coffee room and stopped her. "Montalvo, I know your game," he said condescendingly.

Kathy was taken off guard. "Excuse me?"

He continued, "Play it right, you end up with your picture in the paper, some young brother standing next to you. They'll write about what a hero you are. The chief will give you a commendation. You're just another liberal do-gooder."

Kathy's eyes opened wide. She could not believe what she was hearing.

She calmly responded, "You know detective, I realize I owe you an apology. All this time I thought you were a bigoted, sexist, insensitive chauvinist—when actually, you're really just an overstuffed idiot."

She walked off, leaving Tyler to figure it out, passing Bill Wilson, who had caught enough of the exchange to know what happened.

A few minutes later, Wilson dropped a file at his desk and sat down to review it. Kathy was at her desk, diagonally across the room, on the phone. Through a glass partition, they could see Danny's office.

Kathy was making notes while questioning the caller. "What about priors?"

Danny looked at his watch, then at the photo on his desk of Chris and the dog. He grabbed the phone and dialed. It was his ex-wife's phone number.

Chris answered, heavy metal music filtering through in the background along with other boys' voices. Chris' voice sounded a little slow. Was this something worse than marijuana going on, Danny wondered.

"Lost in a Roman wilderness of pain, all the children are insane." This kind of answer from Chris was not unusual. Chris was unique in all things. The convention of the phone was not to escape his creative mind.

Danny had learned it accomplished nothing to react. "Hey, Chris," he said warmly.

"Dad! How's it?"

"Good." Danny wanted to have a conversation, but it always seemed to start with a question. He tried to make the call sound friendly rather than inquisitive. "So what'a you doing?"

"Shut up, you guys, I can't hear. That's better. What'd you say, Dad?" he asked.

Before Danny could answer, he heard laughter in the background followed by Chris saying, "You're lame! Not you dad.

Danny took the picture of Chris and the shepherd, Thor, in his hand. The younger Chris looked proud next to his handsome and alert dog. After a moment he returned the picture to his desk. Reaching for words, Danny contained his frustration by running his hand through his hair. He looked to see if anyone was watching and then spoke, "Just wondered what you're up to?"

Chris said, "The usual. You know. Hangin' out with my buddies."

"What about the music?"

"It's good," Chris responded.

Danny asked, "You been practicing?"

"Yeah. You guys, shit! Get outta here, will you. Yeah, Dad? What was that?"

Danny swiveled in his chair to face the window, still searching for guidance in dealing with his son. His back was to the door.

"Your mom helping you out?" he asked. Behind him Kathy stopped at the doorway waiting to catch his eye.

"Dad, you don't need to be stressin' on me. I got it under control."

"Right." Having it under control meant Chris was not drunk out of his mind tearing things apart as he had done at his dad's before he was thrown out. To Danny, having it under control meant, a job, school, no drinking, and no drugs.

"Ah, Dad, this isn't the best time for me to be talkin'."

Danny explained, "I was thinking about you. Thought I'd call."

Chris said, "Thinking about you too."

That softened Danny.

"Love you, Chris."

"Love you too, dad."

Danny swiveled back, thoughtfully, set the phone in the cradle, and focused on the picture of his boy. He looked up, noticing Kathy had entered. He was self-conscious wondering what she might have heard.

Danny explained, "My son."

Kathy responded, "Yeah. Déjà vu—twelve years ago. I made my dad nuts. Still do."

Danny winced, "You mean there's hope?"

"With dads like you? Of course!" She was so confident, Danny believed her.

Then he asked, "So, what's up?"

She handed him a form-letter used to notify property owners of a pending investigation. "Is this okay? The way I filled it out?"

He looked at it for a moment. "I need to read this tomorrow," he said.

"No problem," she responded.

Danny began gathering his things as she left the room.

A few minutes later, as Kathy was making a call, Danny walked past her and overheard her phone conversation.

"Hi, Mom. What's for dinner? I need to do some laundry."

That brought a smile to his face as he realized that even at Kathy's age, you bring your laundry home to mom and score a free dinner. Someday he'd be there with Chris bringing home the laundry.

Danny passed Wilson who was carrying two cups of coffee.

"See you later, Bill."

Bill nodded, then stopped him. "Danny, just want to say, Kathy's doing a great job. Good to have her in the unit."

"Thanks for telling me that. That's really good."

Danny continued down the hall as Bill took the coffee back to the office. He put one cup on Kathy's desk without interrupting her file review.

She looked up, "Thanks Bill. How did you know?"

"Experience." Wilson went back to his own desk and the waiting stack of files.

Later that evening, Kathy walked through the front door of her parents' home. It was a nice single-family dwelling south of Olympic Boulevard and just west of Fairfax. The front room had several of Kathy's trophies, photographs and other memorabilia proudly on display.

Kathy had her clothes basket and a container of soap in her arms. Her mom greeted her. "Honey, why did you bring your soap?"

"Habit. When I go to the laundry room I always do."

Kathy put down the basket and hugged her mom as her dad walked in. She turned to him.

"Hi Daddy," she said brightly. "How's my favorite guy?"

He teased, "Still taking abuse from your mother."

Picking up Kathy's basket her mother said to her husband, "Oh, I feel so sorry for you."

Kathy called to her mom, "Hey, I'll do that."

"No. I'll do it. Your dad just got me a new washer, and I'm still having fun trying it out."

He said, "Oh, boy, that thing is so quiet. They just delivered it yesterday."

They moved into the kitchen. Kathy noticed how good the dinner smelled. "Mom, what are you cooking? Is that my favorite chicken Parmesan?"

"Just for you, honey," she replied from the laundry alcove as she started the machine.

"She won't do that for me, you know," her dad joked.

"Oh, Daddy, I know how badly you're treated."

"So, how's the new assignment?" he inquired.

"It's good."

Her mom joined them, and they took seats around the kitchen table next to a bay window that looked out on the backyard.

"Is Hollywood Division any different?" her dad asked.

"No. Well, there's one thing that's happening that I'm really happy about."

"Really. What?" her mom asked.

"My partner, Danny, he and I are coaching some teens in guess what?"

"I wonder whose idea that was?" her dad asked.

"You know me, Daddy. Any reason I can play the game."

But then she got thoughtful. "You know, this is really special. These boys lost their coach. And I know that what we're doing is going to make a difference in their lives."

Mom asked, "How did they lose their coach?"

Kathy shook her head. "Horrible. He was killed by a gang member. It happened right there, on the playground, right after a practice."

Her dad immediately became concerned. "Kathy, are you safe doing that?"

"As safe as I am anywhere, Dad. Things can happen anywhere in this city. I'm sure not going to hide from living. And I am going to give back. You know that's why I joined the department."

"Be careful sweetie, just be careful." He took her hand.

"I am." She looked at her mom and took her hand saying, "Every day, I want to thank you for being so great to me."

They had a wonderful dinner together, as they did every week. It was a ritual Kathy never missed.

CHAPTER 23

Michael was a hard worker. Sanchez had watched him enough to become fond of the teen. In many ways, for the older Mexican, their relationship was developing into one like father and son. Michael had no way to know that. To him, Sanchez was just a nice old guy who spoke with an accent and liked to tell his stories.

John Paul walked through the Sanchez parking lot looking to connect with Michael. Since the day Michael walked off the ball court, they had not spoken. Michael was carrying a bag of trash when JP spotted him.

"Michael! We gotta talk."

Michael kept moving.

JP asked, "Why'd you walk?"

"I don't have time for that practice shit." Michael did not stop. He opened the door to the trash bin and dumped the bag.

"But the game?"

"Look, JP, I ain't down with the team, okay?"

"Oh, you down with Roxanne?"

Michael turned to him. "You don't understand."

"You chilling with her?" JP was demanding to know.

"It's like, shit, that bitch, she rocked my world."

JP wasn't buying the line. "That bitch? Sam tells me she's goin' for the hall of fame."

Michael's anger flared. "What's with you? You gonna school me about bitches? You?"

JP countered, "I ain't chilling with no prosty."

Something came through from JP's eyes and Michael realized his friend was hurt. And he knew JP was not trying to hurt him.

Michael tried to explain. "JP, it's not about you. I got this job—my life—it's screwed. Then there's my mother. I got no time for the hoops. I got Roxanne on my brain, and now there's this other one, Alyssum."

It was a painful moment. JP did not know what to say to his friend. He wanted him back on the courts. He was jealous of the time he assumed Michael was devoting to Roxanne. He understood what Michael dealt with at home and he knew a job was important. Michael glanced at the kitchen, concerned he would get in trouble for stopping his work.

"JP, I gotta go." Michael walked off.

JP blurted out, "We're your friends, Michael. Not some bitch who'll forget your name tomorrow."

Michael looked back at him briefly, then kept on walking.

It was early evening on a Friday. Virginia, John Paul's mother, opened the front door of her house to Kathy. She recognized her immediately.

Seeing the police, Virginia expected trouble. "Something wrong?"

Kathy smiled. "No. I was going to call, but I was in the neighborhood." After a moment she added, "John Paul's really a great kid."

Virginia relaxed her stance. "Thanks. Coming from you, that means something to me. And thanks for what you're doing with him and his friends. He talks about it all the time." Virginia knew that could not be the only reason Kathy was at her front door and she asked, "So, why'd you stop by?"

"Would you have any problem with the team spending a week in the mountains for a basketball tournament this summer?" Kathy asked.

Virginia was surprised.

Kathy explained further, "I don't want to be premature asking, but I thought I'd start with you."

"You really think they have a chance?"

"Absolutely." Kathy's quick response made it clear how much she believed in the boys.

"That would be so..." Virginia interrupted herself. "Why don't you come in?"

Kathy walked inside. "Thanks. I can stay only a minute."

They sat down in the front room.

Wasting no time Virginia said, "I owe you an apology. That night you brought John Paul home, I was pretty mad and, well—I'm sorry. I shouldn't have spoken to you like that."

Kathy smiled. "Don't worry about it. Look, I really want to ask you about John Paul's friend Michael."

"He's a tough one. Is there trouble?" Virginia asked.

"Not exactly. I don't know. He quit the team. I think it upset John Paul."

Virginia looked toward the bedrooms. "Explains his mood tonight. Michael's a kid you want to like."

"You know his parents?" Kathy asked.

"No. I mean I believe that something's not right. Michael is on his own, way too much. Kids. You never know what they're up to. Stay in their face. That's my rule."

Kathy agreed.

Virginia asked, "This tournament. What's it about?"

"If the boys pull together, I think they could qualify and enter. It's a Southern Cal competition drawing kids from all the counties, most summer sports, I think. It would be a great experience for them all. And I really think, if they work hard, they have a chance to get in."

"Would you be the one coaching them at the competition?"

"My detective partner, Danny, he would be with us. We're doing that together."

Virginia nodded. "Well, it sounds like an amazing opportunity for John Paul and the boys. Let me know."

"Thanks. That's good to know."

"I'll help you if I can." Then Virginia asked, "Would you like a glass of wine or I've got soda?"

Kathy noted the time. "Oh, thanks, but I really have to go." Virginia showed her to the door.

As she stepped on the porch, Kathy turned to Virginia, "You've done a great job with John Paul. He's a terrific young man."

Virginia smiled. "Yeah, I think I'll keep him."

After Kathy left, Virginia went to John Paul's room.

He was listening to a CD, shooting baskets with his miniature basketball set as Virginia entered.

"Lose the music for a minute, please," she asked.

JP turned it off and looked back to her, wondering if he was in trouble.

He asked her, "Who were you talking to?"

"Your coach, Kathy."

JP was surprised.

"She's thinking you guys might be able to play in a serious competition. What do you think?"

"Yeah. She mentioned it. We're up for it."

Virginia just nodded. After a moment he read something else in her face.

"What's the matter?" he asked.

"Can we have an honest rap?" she replied.

"What do you mean? I don't lie."

"Honey, that's not what I meant. Look, I know drugs are everywhere today. You'd tell me, wouldn't you?"

"Tell you what?"

"If you were into drugs. I know it's a tough thing to stay out of. God only knows I made my mistakes," she admitted.

JP sat up. "You did drugs?"

"Yes. And I'm not proud of it."

JP was amazed. He had no idea.

"Don't look at me like that. I was a kid once too. That's what I mean when I say I've been there. I survived. And I know it's tougher for you than it was for me."

JP looked up at her with piercing eyes.

Then he asked, "What kind of drugs, mom?"

"I smoked marijuana for a while. Tried a few pills. Stupid stuff. I'm lucky nothing bad happened. Okay. That's the story."

A long moment passed between their eyes.

"I don't do drugs, mom."

"I believe you," she said.

She continued looking at him.

"What?" he asked.

"What's going on with Michael?"

John Paul questioned her. "Why you asking?"

"Hey, it's Friday night and you're here." She said with a kind of sarcasm.

"He's got a job. He's not down with the team. Him and me talked."

"He and I..."

"Whatever. Mom, I don't want to do this, okay?"

She knew it was better to give him some space. She turned for the door. "Okay. Be in bed by eleven."

"It's Friday night, remember?"

Virginia relented. "Twelve."

He turned away from her as she pulled the door closed. He turned the music back up and resumed the basketball, expressionless. He tossed his miniature basketball at the hoop over the wastebasket and swished one.

JP couldn't help wondering what Michael was doing. For three years, Friday nights had been their sacred time. School was done for the week. They could stay up later. Sometimes they caught a movie, grabbed a burger, got out in the night. But without him JP had no interest in stepping out. So he took another shot at the hoop, and made a basket.

Kathy walked into her second-floor apartment in the Hollywood Hills. It was on Beachwood Drive, in the canyon that jutted out from the hills that held the famous landmark sign. Her building was a French Chateau architectural beauty. It had been built in the '30s and was a choice place to live.

Kathy liked order and space. The walls were pure white with little art. The floors were wood, polished, and reflective of the white perimeter. The collection of hardcover novels stacked three feet high along one of the walls made it evident that she liked to read. There were books from Joseph Campbell, a full collection of Shakespeare, nineteenth-century classics, art reference books including her favorite college text, *History of Art,* by H.W. Janson.

Hanging in the center of that wall were a Lakota Sioux symbol of prayer—a wooden arrow with a tobacco pouch tied to it; a bear-claw necklace, a symbol of power and wisdom; and perhaps what she viewed as most critical, the middle feather of an owl, a symbol of balance and harmony.

At the center of the opposite wall was a simple mahogany Butsudan, a small unadorned wooden encasement similar in purpose to a tabernacle. It held her Gohonzon: a mandala in the form of a scroll with Chinese and Sanskrit characters that expressed the Dharma, the universal law that, in Buddhism, permeated life. This was her place of prayer every morning and evening. Kathy was devoted to Nichiren Buddhism, a particular school of the ancient religion established about 752 years ago in Japan. She believed strongly in an essential element of the practice: strength of one's faith.

Kathy had followed Nichiren Buddhism since her teen years. It was brought into her life by her high school coach. Later, she had found it no coincidence that the famous NBA coach Phil Jackson had adopted the precepts of Zen Buddhism, which inspired his unorthodox methods of coaching his world champion Chicago Bulls, or that her favorite musician, the brilliant jazz pianist Herbie Hancock, practiced Nichiren Buddhism.

Kathy put her purse down, lit candles on each side of the Gohonzon, lit incense, and took up her prayer beads, then sat very erect in the black lacquered eighteenth-century French side chair she reserved for this twice daily ritual of Gongyo. Then she subtly rang a bell to begin her offering of prayer, bowed and began to chant "Nam-myoho-renge-kyo."

On the sidewalk below a Swedish man was walking his Siberian husky. He could hear Kathy's chant and looked up to the window listening. The dog looked too, heard the chant, and began a soft howl.

The man leaned over and stroked her. "Sounds nice, huh? You want to chant, girl?"

The husky looked at him and then pulled him forward to continue their evening walk.

CHAPTER 24

Messy clutter surrounded Alicia. She was on the couch channel surfing. A half-eaten pizza sat in a box on the coffee table alongside a half-empty pint of cheap whiskey. Her hair matched the environment, dirty and unkempt.

She stopped the channel on wrestling. Two steroid casualties with slicked-back hair were trying to get the better of each other.

The front door opened and Michael walked in.

He noticed the mess, but ignored it as best he knew how. "Hi, Mom," he said with concern.

"Why are you late?"

"I was working," he replied defensively.

"Oh, yeah. So, you want some dinner? Pizza here."

She changed channels, stopping on a baseball game. Michael took a seat, considered the cold pizza and quickly decided to pass. He took his eyes off the mess on the table and looked at the TV just as a black player hit a home run. The crowd cheered, but the channel changed. It stopped on a basketball game. A black player took a three-point shot and the ball swished in.

Alicia piped up. "See that? You got the wrong color skin."

Michael got up.

Alicia looked up at him and asked, "Where you going?"

"Meeting a friend."

"Not till you get the trash picked up."

"I do that all day," he said angrily. "And this isn't my mess. Why don't you clean it up?"

Alicia was not going to listen to backtalk. "Do your part around here."

He sighed, knowing there was no point in arguing. As he picked up the clutter, Alicia asked, "Did you get paid today?"

"Why?" he asked.

"Let me borrow twenty. My check didn't come."

"But I don't have very much," he pleaded.

"You got a job—you help me out." She put out her hand.

Michael reached in his pocket and pulled out his crumpled fold of bills. He handed her a twenty. She could not look in his eyes. After a moment he headed to the kitchen with the trash, and bundled it in a large bag. He carried it out the front door, departing without a comment to, or from his mother. She looked to the door as it closed, and then dropped her head. Her shame was overridden by a paralysis gripping her in the alcoholic state of mind she lived in. The bottle seemed to be the only solution, in that moment.

High school kids formed a holding line while waiting to be admitted to Liquid, the club all the hip young kids wanted to get into—now. It featured live music on Saturday nights.

Michael passed faces, looking for Roxanne. The same look repeated boy after boy and girl after girl. It was the cool scene—cleavage, makeup, tight pants, cigarettes, pierced tongues, tattoos, and colored hair.

At the door a bouncer picked the lucky ones, always the sexy girls and anyone with them. Michael was looking, not knowing how he would get inside. Finally he moved back to the rear of the line. He felt awkward standing there alone.

After a few moments Roxanne and two of her girlfriends walked by. Roxanne was stoned, smoking a cigarette when she saw Michael.

"Hey, Michael. You showed."

"Yeah." He was relieved that she was there. "Got us a place in line."

Roxanne looked at him like he was nuts. "I don't wait for dick."

She walked off and he followed.

At the door the bouncer recognized her and let her pass with her two friends and Michael.

They stepped into a flat-black hallway that led to a cashier. As Roxanne passed the cashier she gave the manager, a slick looking man about forty, a more-than-friendly hug and kiss. She never looked back for Michael, but rather continued on with her two friends. The manager stopped Michael.

"Forty," he said to Michael.

"What?" Michael had no idea what was up.

"Four of you. Ten apiece. The price of fame, stud."

"Oh. Just a second." Michael reached in his pocket and counted his money. He had a pair of twenties and a five. Then Michael looked into the club. It was glamorous to his callow eyes. There it was, the edge of the stage, the band, the lights, the smoke, the people, and especially there was Roxanne. She looked really hot. She was right at home. Michael wanted that scene. It was too cool, right out of a movie. He took a deep breath, peeled off forty, and put Abe Lincoln back in his pocket.

The cashier took the money, and the club manager motioned for him to go in.

Michael politely said, "Thanks."

"Move it along, will you sport," the manager said.

Michael worked his way through the crowd. In the background the band was at full power, electrifying the room. The dance floor was packed, bodies moving, grinding, banging, slamming.

Roxanne appeared in Michael's face, laughing. She was lit by a flashing strobe so he caught wild-looking, stop-motion-like images of her. Roxanne had a colored balloon that she was taking big hits from.

Michael's eyes were wide. The whole scene was almost overwhelming. Roxanne pushed her body up against his, rubbing. He didn't know whether to dance or what.

She asked him, "Do you feel as good as you look?"

She put her arms around his neck and planted a lip lock on him. She was so stoned and happy from the gas she was inhaling she did not realize how nervous he was.

He did not like the kiss. She pulled back and gave him a seductive, heavy-eyed look. Then she took him by the hand and led him across the room. They passed what seemed like hundreds of bodies wound up together on the dance floor.

The door from the club to the alley opened, and Roxanne led Michael into the shadows of a basement stairwell alongside the building. She placed him one step below her so he was eye level with her breasts. Then she started to unbutton his shirt, working her fingers on his chest. As she felt his tense chest muscles, she was rubbing her leg in his crotch.

This was hot, Michael thought, his body temperature rising with every touch of her fingers and motion of her leg. But he was nervous about doing this outside, in plain sight. His eyes were watching for anything that might move. Then she felt his shirt pocket and seemed surprised.

"Where'd you hide it, Michael?" she asked.

"What?"

"The Ecstasy," she said.

"I don't have any," he replied.

She stopped her seductive moves and turned cold.

"You what?" she demanded.

"I just thought we could just hang," he said innocently.

She straightened up and walked away as if he had vanished.

Michael was stunned. "Roxanne?"

She did not react, but kept up her cool pace right to the side door. Michael went after her, but the door closed before he got to it. He tried to open it, but the door was locked. He banged on it, but no one responded.

At the front door, Michael tried to pass the bouncer but was stopped dead in his tracks.

The bouncer collared Michael. "Hey, what the hell you doin', asshole?"

"I already paid. I been in there." Michael was gesturing in the hallway. He caught a glimpse of the manager.

Michael sputtered, "Him, he knows. He called me sport."

"Yeah, right. You got ID?"

Michael could only say, "No."

The bouncer pushed him back. "Get outta here, asshole."

Michael looked around. Everyone in the line was watching him. Totally humiliated, he walked off.

CHAPTER 25

ALONE

Michael walked across the Fifth Street Bridge. The structure was a concrete landmark of the noir days of Los Angeles. It spanned the L.A. River and the Southern Pacific railroad tracks seventy feet below. For Angelenos the bridge kept the old days alive. Starting four blocks west, the downtown skyline rose into an overcast sky on that evening. A marine-induced moisture-laden air gave the night a peculiar atmosphere.

Light auto traffic was passing close by as Michael stopped alongside one of the parapets that guarded the bridge. A quarter-mile away an Amtrak train approached, its main headlights cutting through the slight haze that softened the view of the rail yard below.

Michael looked at the approaching train. The shaft of light projected from the engine had a mesmerizing effect on him. He climbed to the top of the parapet's concrete handrail and precariously rose to his full height. Extending his arms he began inching his way around the perimeter. The train was getting closer, its track line cutting directly under him.

A car passed behind Michael, its young passengers let out a whistle and a catcall of encouragement as he continued to inch his way, oblivious of his audience. The train, now very close, sounded its horn. He seemed enthralled by the rapidly approaching train.

Michael's face was blank. Time had stopped as he looked into that black cavern right in front of him. Was that eternity he wondered, all that black space out there? And there was the light beam from the train looking as if it would support his steps. He could just hold his arms out and float in that heavy air right to the light shaft.

Michael began to reach for the light with his fingers. The train's horn sounded again. The light was getting closer. Michael could hear the engine. Its horn called again. He could read the engine numbers it was so close: 1602. He watched his hands against the backdrop of the approaching train.

Suddenly he heard a voice say, "That which dies is born."

He almost fell as he looked back. The old homeless man from the alley was passing on the sidewalk. The man moved through the night, passing by with a purpose only he could comprehend. He vanished as quickly as he had appeared, much like the train did every evening as it headed south.

Michael's hands hit the chain-link fencing around the playground swimming pool hard enough that the galvanized links slapped the support pipes, causing them to ring. As the bright tone faded, only his heavy breathing filled his ears.

Michael climbed the fence and with no hesitation he stripped his clothes off and walked to the pool's edge. The dark blue surface was a mirror in the gray sky and held those alluring qualities he had felt minutes earlier on the bridge.

For Michael there was a comfort in what he heard underwater. That muted world of sound provided an escape from his universe. Following the contour of the bottom felt natural to him. He could effortlessly manage two minutes without another breath. He broke the surface on his dive and cut a path to the bottom. He swam the length enveloped in liquid silence, descending to the twelve-foot deep end, where he executed a turn and then with ease returned to the shallow end.

Michael rose to the surface and filled his aching lungs. He grasped the edge and lifted himself out. He had leaned down to pick up his clothes when he heard the words.

"Want to play one on one, Michael?" It was Art's voice.

Michael snapped his head toward the voice. Nothing. He looked the other direction. Nothing but the night shared his space. He grabbed his clothes and walked to a corner that offered some shelter.

Michael sat back against the wall. He pulled his legs close against his chest, wrapping his arms around them. Then he rested his forehead on his knees.

Above Michael, five hundred yards north, the red CNN sign glowed, its colors bleeding into the light fog.

The following day had arrived and the activity of the playground included Danny, Kathy, John Paul, Alonzo, Sam, and Anthony painting out graffiti on the rec room. On Cole Avenue a patrol car stopped a rap-booming car.

A little while later on the sidelines of the ball court, the boys, complete with paint splotches on their hands, arms and faces, gathered around Kathy and Danny. She pulled a bright yellow jersey from a bag. It was emblazoned with dark blue letters reading, "Hollywood PAL HAWKS."

The boys were more than surprised as Kathy and Danny tossed jerseys to each of them. They ripped off their T-shirts, donning their new jerseys amid much excitement.

Kathy tossed one to Danny. "I even got these for you and me."

Kathy pulled out a T-shirt with "Coach" stitched on it. He looked it over and proudly put it on.

"Who came up with the Hawks?" Alonzo asked.

"It's perfect. You're all ball hawks," she replied.

Sam added, "It's cool, you know what I'm sayin'."

"Yeah," JP agreed.

"I'm down with these jerseys," added Anthony.

"Okay! Team, the next stop is the summer competition!" Kathy exclaimed.

The boys erupted with a combination of high-fives and slappin' skins.

Danny interrupted their elation. "But we still need low post. Anyone know someone who can play pivot?"

Sam answered, "Damn, Michael. You know what I'm sayin'?"

Kathy followed with, "You guys see who you can recruit. So, JP, what about Michael?"

JP was quick to say, "He's a loser."

Off the court about one hundred yards away Michael stood in the shade of a tree, watching his team. He was too far away to hear the words, but he could see what was going down.

Danny grabbed their attention. "All right. Enough jawing, let's play."

The boys broke off into a practice routine, following each other in a loop, each one making a layup. Then they broke into a semicircle around the top of the key. Danny and Kathy watched them from under the backboard as they each took three-point shots. JP made his, Anthony missed, Sam's almost went down but rolled out. Alonzo's shot dropped in like it had eyes.

"Lonzo hits the money shot!" JP said with great pride.

The boys exchanged another round of high-fives.

Kathy turned to Danny. "They actually look like a team."

Danny looked a little overwhelmed by that truth. "Yeah. They do."

A few moments later he added, "I have these moments, wondering why I can't do this with my own kid."

He knew there was no answer to that question. He could only hope that by staying in the game of life with his son, their lives would evolve to a place of mutual understanding and respect. He wanted his son to feel purpose in living, to realize what joy could come from putting forth an effort directed at a lofty goal. Success was as much in the effort as it was in the achievement of the goal, Danny believed.

For Michael it would be a long walk home. As he moved down the block, a breeze worked its way along the treetops. He could have been a part of all that team energy. Instead he was alone and more convinced than ever that he was a loser.

CHAPTER 26

The nights on Sunset Boulevard were all action. Michael loved it all: the cruisers passing by in thick traffic, the sidewalks with the menagerie on display coming and going out of clubs, restaurants, record stores, and hotels. He stepped from Virgin's megastore and looked in each direction and walked to a Starbucks down the block.

The patio was crowded with teens. They were all the cool ones, like Roxanne. Michael looked around and spotted her. She was in tight jeans with lots of cleavage showing and those hoopties dangling along her jaw line.

He walked up to her but she ignored him, continuing her conversation with two girlfriends. They were talking in a lot of syllables that had numerous OOOOs added to prepositions and descriptive words with the result being "soooo cooool."

Finally she turned to him, munching on a Kit-Kat. "Whassup, Michael?"

Her eyes were wandering everywhere.

He tried to be cool but that was impossible in this circumstance. Michael had yet to learn that in the game played by the Roxannes of the world, there was no way to win. When the Michaels are no longer intriguing or do not have what the Roxanne types want, the Michael types are history. This phenomenon of the heart is not exclusive to gender, but it is exclusive to personality type. Pursuit of a self-centered individual equates with slamming one's head against a wall of stone. The act can only result in pain.

Awkwardly he said, "Just lookin' for you."

Roxanne cocked her head. "You need to be schooled." She was looking right into his eyes as she continued, "Join a crew. C-R-E-A-M. Cream, Michael. Cash rules everything around me."

Her eyes studied him. "My parents, they got plenty of money. But me, I lay down my duckets for nothing. Know why?"

He had no clue. He felt stripped wide open. This girl had X-ray eyes.

She went on. "'Cause I got dick. That's like, someday you got balls, maybe. Fall in with a crew and learn, Michael. A little CC." She lit a cigarette and added, "You don't know what I'm sayin'."

Michael now felt as if everyone on the patio was listening to them. He could say nothing.

"How old are you?" she asked.

"Fifteen."

Roxanne blew him off with, "Go home, Michael. Grow up before you try to play in the yard with the big kids."

She walked off, cozying up to a guy about eighteen wearing leather pants and a motorcycle jacket.

Michael crossed the street wanting to get far away. The silence of the pool water would have been warm compared to the ice queen who had just ripped him open. Embarrassed in a patio full of cool people. What a great night he was having. He pushed his way past a boy and a girl his age who were blocking the sidewalk in front of a corner liquor store. Crack was stepping out of the store, and they almost collided.

Crack blurted out, "Watch the shoes!"

Michael slowed and sincerely said, "Sorry, dude."

He continued on his way. Crack could not believe Michael was not his normal confrontational self.

He called out, "Boy. Come here!"

Michael stopped and turned. After a moment Crack walked over to him.

"What's with you?" Crack asked.

"Nothin'."

Crack did not buy it. He looked him up and down.

"Still got your, job?"

"Yeah."

"Interested in real money yet?"

Michael thought for a moment. His mind was still on Roxanne so he looked over his shoulder. He spotted Roxanne hanging on the guy's arm as they moved down the sidewalk to a motorcycle. Michael looked back to Crack, who had also noticed this.

Michael responded, "Yeah, I'm interested."

Crack smiled. "That's good, my man. I could use you tonight. You up for that?"

The motorcycle across the street started. As the driver pulled away, he hung a U-turn and wound its tight engine to 8000 RPMs. Michael looked to see Roxanne with her arms wrapped around the guy's waist. The motorcycle sped past them and down the block.

Green with envy, Michael turned to Crack. "Yeah. I'm more than ready."

Crack nodded. "Guess you are. Okay, follow me."

As they walked, Michael took another look at the motorcycle as it made a left turn and disappeared.

He looked at Crack and asked, "Dude, you know what CC means?"

"CC! Credit card scammin'. Why you wanna know?"

"Just wonderin'."

Crack did not believe Michael's answer. "That bitch, she talkin' that shit with you?"

"No, dude. I heard someone say it and was wonderin'."

Crack knew better. "Bitches like that. All the same."

CHAPTER 27

Danny still held his keys. He had entered through the backdoor off the patio, just a few steps from the alley facing garage. It was dark at the front of his house, but a sliver of light came through Poppi's bedroom door. Danny could hear his dad softly snoring. He carefully closed the door and walked toward the front room. At that moment he heard something coming from the kitchen: Someone was in the house. He drew his service revolver and carefully moved forward.

The glow coming in the front window from the porch lamp gave Chris just enough light. He was sifting through papers in a kitchen drawer. Danny flipped on the light, gun pointed at the intruder.

"Dad!" Chris said, startled.

"What are you doing in here?" Danny said, just as startled. He holstered his pistol. He was rattled by what could have happened. "I might have shot you!"

"You scared me!" said Chris as he regained his composure. "Sorry, I thought you were asleep."

"What are you looking for?" Danny's tone was firm.

"I didn't want to bother you. I just need the receipt for my amp, Dad."

"This couldn't wait till morning?" Danny walked over to the refrigerator and took out a soft drink. "And what do you need it for?"

"I made a deal on a better one. The guy wants to trade now."

"Well the receipt's not there, and I'd appreciate it if you put those papers back, as you found them."

Chris nodded. "Sure." He started straightening the papers and asked, "So could you get it for me?"

Danny thought about it for a second. "It's somewhere in my files in the garage. I'm tired, Chris."

"I'll look for it."

"No! I don't want anyone digging in my shit. You can wait till tomorrow." Danny was really hot.

"Chill, dad."

Danny snapped. "Chill yourself. You sneak in my house, asking favors."

"This used to be my house too," said Chris.

"You gave up the privilege after you broke your bedroom door. You wanna talk about that?"

Chris held up his hands in a stopping motion.

"I know, I know. I was drunk. I'm an alcoholic, remember?"

"Oh, please. Don't try that line on me again."

Chris began to withdraw.

Holding up his hands, Chris said, "I'm sorry. About everything, okay. I know I'm not wanted here."

Danny sighed.

Chris pleaded, "Please, Dad. I gotta do things my way, even if you think it's nuts. It's my life, it's my pain."

Danny was cooling off and reason was taking over from emotion. "You don't live it alone."

A long silence followed as Danny looked at his son.

"Come back in the morning. We'll find it. You can have breakfast with Poppi. Make him real happy."

Chris responded, "Maybe." He finished with the papers and closed the drawer. "Dad, you got a couple of bucks? I'm out of cigarettes."

Danny instinctively began to reach in his pocket, then stopped. "No. I won't do that anymore."

Chris nodded. "I understand."

Chris walked out of the kitchen and headed to the front door.

Danny called to him, "Be careful."

The front door closed. Danny watched through the window as Chris walked off.

"I love you, son," Danny said. He knew Chris could not hear the words in that moment. Saying the phrase, however, carried a promise of a future time that he desperately wanted for both of them.

CHAPTER 28

Michael and Crack were lampin' across the street from an all-night convenience store on Santa Monica Boulevard. The store, set back from the curb by its parking lot, was in a seedy area with barred windows on all the buildings and little life on the street after sunset.

Crack checked the time, then looked down the street.

Michael asked, "So what kind of job is it?"

"Deliverin' some goods. But I gotta do some business over there first."

Michael nodded and started toward the other side of the street just as a sedan turned into the store's parking lot.

Crack noticed the car and said, "No, you hang here." Crack moved across the street. Michael watched him cross the parking lot and approach the car that had just parked. Suddenly feeling conspicuous, he moved himself out from under the street lamp and against the wall of the building, out of the light.

The old man from the bridge stepped up to Michael from the darkness, his eyes wild. "That which dies is born."

The words frightened Michael and made no sense. Once again the crazy-looking old man disappeared into the shadows. Michael felt even more vulnerable on the street. He looked across the street and could see Crack talking to the driver, still sitting behind the wheel.

After a moment Crack walked into the store, and the car turned into the street pulling to a stop in front of Michael.

"Hey, you Michael?" the driver called out.

Michael looked inside the car. He had no way of realizing the driver was Danny's son, Chris.

Michael said, "Yeah."

"Crack said you should wait with me."

Michael was glad to be getting off the street.

As Michael settled in the front passenger seat Chris said, "Name's Chris." He reached out and they did the handgrip thing.

Michael asked, "You with Crack?"

"Trading some stuff with him."

They both turned silent. Michael looked over toward the convenience store. He was getting more uncomfortable by the moment. Chris began tapping out a drum rhythm on the steering wheel with his lightning-fast hands. He stopped, pulling out a pack of Marlboro Reds and offered one to Michael.

Michael responded, "No, thanks."

Chris lit up, took a drag, then coughed a little. "I gotta start workin' out again, give up the grits."

More silence. Chris beat out another rhythm.

"So whadda you do, Mike?"

"Basketball, work."

"Oh, yeah. What about school?"

"I do that too."

"That's cool. Basketball. My dad loves basketball."

Things turned quiet again. Then suddenly they both heard what sounded like a gunshot, then running footsteps.

Michael and Chris both snapped their heads around and saw Crack in a dead run toward them.

A man yelled out, "You! Stop!"

The man was running from the store across the parking lot and chasing Crack. The man was a solitary image, backlit from the store-front lights and pointing a pistol in his hand.

Crack yelled, "Start the car!"

The man aimed at Crack and fired, hitting him in the back. Crack fell forward onto the car, his face pressed up against the left rear window. His eyes were dead, but they stared at Michael. His body slid slowly to the ground.

Chris was freaked. "What the...?" He tried to start the car. He turned the key, grinding the starter while desperately trying to get the motor running. Michael was in complete terror. The man from the parking lot kept running toward the car, the gun pointing at both boys.

Michael screamed, "He's coming!"

Chris got the car in gear and floored it. The wheels squealed. The man was almost on them when he fired a shot. Chris was rounding the corner as the back window shattered. Michael hit the floorboard, taking cover.

The car sped along with Chris driving radically. Fortunately for both boys, neither was hit by the gunshot.

Michael, in shock, peeked over the seatback and said, "Did you see Crack's face?"

"No, I was looking at the wigged-out freak firing at us."

Michael said, "This was supposed to be a job."

Chris yelled, "Shit! I just wanted to score some bud. That's all. My mom's car—I'm screwed."

Just then revolving red lights came on from an approaching police car.

Chris realized the situation was going from very bad to worse with every rotation of the approaching lights. "Oh, shit!" he yelled.

They passed the police unit and held their breaths, hoping it would not turn. But it hung a U-turn and raced up behind them, its siren blaring.

"What's going down?" Michael said to himself.

Another set of red lights appeared in front of them, then a third set. The roadway was blocked. The boys had nowhere to go.

Chris yelled, "Shit! What do I do?"

Michael screamed, "Stop, fool!"

Chris slammed on the brakes, the front of the car diving down toward the pavement as the car slid, stopping just before hitting the patrol cars.

Intense light poured into the car on Michael and Chris through both the front and rear windows. All Michael could see were guns.

Through a bullhorn the boys heard, "Put your hands on the dashboard!" It was so loud it seemed the voice reverberated through both of them.

Michael's face was ashen. Chris said simply, "Life's over."

CHAPTER 29

INSIDE

D anny and Kathy were talking about ten feet from Michael and Chris. The boys were sitting together in a holding cell.

Chris spoke softly, addressing himself. "He'll kill me." After a moment he spoke to Chris. "That man. He's my dad."

Michael shook his head. "But he's—"

Chris interrupted. "A cop!"

Michael responded. "He's my coach. Basketball."

Chris wanted to bury himself. "This keeps getting worse. Please, make it stop," he said, praying.

Kathy walked away through a hallway. Danny was looking at the cell, and saw Chris with his hands clasped in prayer mode. Stepping to the bars, his eyes locked on Chris. "You're a little late with that."

Danny never looked at Michael. He walked away, opened a door and disappeared. The door was metal, and it had a very cold and permanent quality to its sound.

The boys felt the cold reality of being behind bars. They felt a chill through their bones, their mouths got dry, their stomachs turned over and they knew that they would do anything, make any promise, change everything in their lives, just to have the chance to turn the clock back so that they were not facing those steel bars and all this place meant.

Their eyes darted from cell to cell in the small jail holding area. Two hard-looking men were being placed in a cell across the way.

There was momentary eye contact, enough to chase Chris' and Michael's eyes somewhere else.

Chris wondered if anyone in this place would realize, or even care, that he was really a nice guy who never wanted to hurt anyone. But how could they know? He was behind bars. And not for a speeding ticket or DUI. Someone was dead. He began to understand the meaning of something he had heard his dad say many times. When the law looks through the bars at a prisoner or the court looks down from the bench, they don't see any difference, one criminal to another. They do not know anything more than they see. They have no reason to figure that you are really not a criminal. Everyone looks the same in jailhouse clothes.

Michael wondered about his mother. Would she miss him? How would he explain this? But Danny and Kathy would listen, he thought. They would understand that he was innocent. They could explain it. They had to explain it. But why would they? Michael had dismissed them, he did not want anything to do with them. He left his friends behind because he wanted to impress Roxanne. He did not want to talk with Kathy because she was a Penelope.

An hour passed. To the boys, it seemed like an entire night. Then Detective Tyler came to the cell with a uniformed officer. He took Michael first, leaving Chris to himself.

Michael was taken to the same room in which John Paul had been interrogated. He was left in the room, alone with the mirrored window, which showed his reflection. He did not like seeing himself but was afraid to get up and move. Tyler had told him to sit and wait for the D.A. Michael had seen enough of "The Shield" and "NYPD Blue" to know what the "D.A." meant. He was in big trouble.

Tyler went back with the officer and called Chris out of the cell. As he stepped from the bars, Chris politely asked, "Can I see my dad?"

Tyler responded, "Shut up and follow me."

The officer brought up the rear as the trio walked the corridor. They passed eyes from inside the holding cells that watched them. Those were nameless faces to Chris. And he was a nameless face to them.

They put Chris in the room that George had been interrogated in. The uniformed officer stood by the door as Tyler sat down at the end of the table to Chris' right. Chris was facing the window. A moment passed in silence.

Chris tried again, "My dad's a detective. Can I please . . ."

Tyler cut him off. "I advise you to say nothing."

Chris looked away from Tyler, who was not looking at him but at the door. Tyler looked hard and tough. When Tyler had just spoken, Michael noticed the scar on his right hand and wondered how he got it.

Another moment passed, and Wilson, who was wearing a coat and tie, walked in carrying a pad. He took a seat directly opposite Chris. Wilson made a few notes on the top of page such as date, time, who was present in the room with him.

Before he began his interrogation he said to Tyler in quiet tones, "Remember that 16-year-old in officer Jackson's murder, George Dupre?" Tyler looked at him and nodded. "He's being tried as an adult for first-degree murder."

Chris did not connect this to his dad's friend Art. But he had heard that a sixteen-year-old was being tried as an adult for murder.

Tyler coldly replied, "Good. One less of these assholes on the streets."

Wilson turned to Chris. "For the record my name is Detective

Wilson, this is Detective Tyler and that is Officer Jones."

Chris leaned forward a little and said, "My dad is—"

Tyler cut him off again. "Detective Wilson is asking the questions. You answer them. Otherwise, keep your mouth shut."

Wilson looked at Chris, who was becoming concerned and added, "You'll do a lot better in here if you do as you are told. Now, state your name, place of birth, age, and your current address."

Inside the observation room Danny was standing with Kathy. Kathy had a little smile on her face.

She turned to Danny. "You are wicked."

He responded, "First time I ever liked the way Tyler handled a prisoner. Maybe they'll scare some sense into the little shit."

The boys were interrogated in grand style. Wilson was having fun being a straight man to Tyler's normal tough routine. They went back and forth from room to room comparing notes on the boys with one purpose. They were carrying on a lesson in helplessness, the point being that these two had placed themselves in harm's way. They did it without giving any thought to the consequences of who they were with, where they were, or what was happening on that fateful evening.

When Danny and his colleagues figured the boys had learned something, he had them placed in the same room. Michael and Chris sat opposite a very angry Danny, who stood across from them.

"How long have you two half-wits known each other?"

Michael offered, "We just met." Chris nodded.

Danny went on. "What the hell were you two thinking?"

They started to answer, but he cut them off.

"I don't want to hear it. Hanging out with a scumbag! You could be dead, in a body bag in the morgue. Do you know that the bullet that took out the rear window of the car missed you geniuses by inches? You want to bet your life on inches? Do you get it?"

Chris said, "Absolutely."

Michael nodded, "Yes."

Danny went on, "Or what's worse, you could be charged as accomplices. You idiots know what that means?"

Danny began to pace. They did not know how to answer.

"Armed robbery! Or what if that scumbag killed someone?"

He stopped and stared at them with an intensity that pinned them into their chair backs. "By the time you're out of prison, life's over. Felons. It stays on your record, forever. And everywhere you go, anytime you try to do anything, people will find out that you were in prison.

Danny looked at them, motionless for a moment, his eyes darting back and forth between the two wide-eyed boys.

Danny looked at his son. "Chris, I'm done. I've had it with

your bullshit. Deal with your mother about the car. It's in the impound yard. When they release you, walk. Don't expect me to give you a ride."

Chris was afraid to speak as Danny stared hard at him. He finally managed, "I understand."

Danny continued looking at Chris while talking to Michael.

"Michael, I'm taking you home. I need to speak with your parents."

Neither of the boys moved. They were waiting to be told it was okay to stand. They jumped when Danny barked, "Now!"

CHAPTER 30

PLEASE, MOM

For both Michael and Chris, the weather set the backdrop for the picture-perfect finale to a wretched night. Rain was sheeting off the windshield of Danny's Explorer. No radio, no wind noise, no conversation, just the sound of the wipers and torrential rain filled the car as Michael sat, waiting for a light to change at the intersection. Danny's silence made things worse. All Michael could now think about was his mother and that he did not want to see her.

The light changed and Danny crossed the intersection with caution. It was not what Alicia was going to say to Michael that concerned him, but rather, what Danny would think of her. What would this man think of his mother? Michael hoped and prayed that she was not drunk tonight. His thoughts were interrupted when Danny suddenly spoke.

"You know, Michael, I watched you walk away from your friends on the team, and here I am driving you home from the police station in the middle of the night. Does that tell you anything? It tells me something. Want to know what? This whole thing tonight was your choice."

Michael felt he had to defend himself. He really wanted to explain, to find some way to avoid the simple fact just stated by Danny. Somehow, in his naïve thoughts, his actions were exclusive and did not connect to anything beyond his intention. The understanding of his personal responsibility had not struck him when he said, "I didn't do anything to get arrested for."

"You hung out with Crack. It was your choice to be with him when he committed a felony."

"I didn't know he had a gun, was gonna rob a store."

Danny responded. "Doesn't matter. If he had killed the storeclerk and you were with him when he drove away, you would be an accessory to the crime of murder. And, by the way, we wouldn't be driving home right now. You'd be in custody for a long time. And your next basketball game would be with boys dressed in blue with numbers printed on the backs of their state-issued uniform shirts."

The car came to a stop at a red light.

"I know. I screwed up. Believe me, I get it. I really get it," Michael said sincerely. Danny sensed something really important, something he wanted to hear. Michael was taking responsibility.

"I hope you do, Michael. I really do."

The light changed and Danny started across the intersection.

Danny continued, "Make the wrong choices now, there's no way out."

A dark image suddenly appeared in the crosswalk on the other side of the intersection. Danny slammed on the brakes stopping just short of a pedestrian. A bolt of lightning turned the sky to electric blue for a moment. As the old man turned toward the windshield Michael realized that this was the old man he had seen before. The lightning struck again, and the old man appeared like an image projected out of the sky, pointing at Michael. He was saying those words, understood only by Michael.

Danny said, "Crazy fool! Get out of the crosswalk." He honked the horn, and the old man disappeared. Danny drove on, but Michael was still in the moment, still seeing the image of the lightning and the old man. Those words, "That which dies is born" rang in his ears.

They went a few more blocks in silence. Then Michael spoke. "JP'll never forgive me for walking."

Danny asked, "You tried talking to him?"

"No."

"You should," Danny said encouragingly. The balance of the trip to Michael's apartment was in silence.

Michael and Danny passed the apartment manager as they made their way toward the boy's apartment. The manager was a wiry man, mid-50s, bald, a little smelly, and generally unpleasant. The hallway of this older building offered an odor made up of years of tenants' meals, the smells that would find their way under several doors and permeate hallways. The manager's shirt carried some of that fragrance and the toothpick he was preoccupied with suggested the meal was recent.

He tapped Michael on the arm. "Boy, tell your mother, I want the rent. Understand?"

"Yes." Michael continued on immediately. He was embarrassed and expecting the worst when he went into his apartment. The manager barely made eye contact with Danny before he walked on.

Alicia unlocked the deadbolt, opening the door to Danny and Michael. She looked at them both, said not one word, turned and walked back to the sofa. Alicia looked blankly at the TV, her disheveled apartment surrounding her.

Danny followed Michael in and closed the door. Trying not to react to the conditions, he took a seat opposite Alicia. Michael sat to her left.

Without looking she asked, "What's he done?"

Danny took his time answering. The environment had his attention. Alicia noticed.

She quipped, "I gave the maid the year off."

Michael interceded. "Mom? He's a friend, my basketball coach."

Alicia looked at Michael. "You told me the team was finished."

Danny was getting a picture of Michael's life and stepped in. "We started it again."

Alicia looked at Danny, still wondering why he was here.

Danny took a deep breath, put on a smile and said, "I want your permission for Michael to join his team for a week of competition in the mountains."

Michael's eyes went wide. Did he actually hear what he thought he heard? Alicia stared at the television giving no comment.

Michael jumped in. "Mom! Please."

Alicia's attention stayed on the television. Danny looked at the screen to see what was so compelling. It was a rerun of "Married…With Children." He glanced at Michael, who was waiting for his mother's response. Five minutes earlier Danny had been prepared to let Michael's parents know about their son's activities that eventful evening. But the agenda changed somewhere between the hallway and the television. In that time, as the sitcom showed teenage characters making fun of their father, Danny wondered why he suddenly felt a need to be tolerant. Was it his continued feeling of failure with Chris that gripped him in the moment he asked Alicia's permission for Michael to join the team?

Danny maintained his composure and spoke again. "This is an opportunity he may never have again. He's a gifted athlete, Mrs. Ahern."

"I need him here," she said flatly.

"Mom, I'll take care of everything."

Danny added, "Look, if it's about the cost"......

It was the first time Alicia looked at Danny, and she cut him off mid-sentence. "The cost? I can't pay my rent, the electricity's gonna be shut off. And you think some game's important to me?"

Danny stated frankly, "It's probably the best thing you could do for your son. Anyway, there is no cost. Everything is covered."

Alicia looked over at Michael, processing what she had just heard. After a moment, her edge dulled slightly.

Then she softened. "You play that good, honey?"

"Yeah, I do." He was anxious, more so than ever.

She looked at Danny again for a moment before speaking. "You look like a good person. Okay."

Michael was at Alicia's side in a flash and gave her a hug.

"You should see me play, Mom."

"I'd like to—sometime." She was convincing as she spoke those words. She knew she was doing something right for a change. Her permission had come as an expression of love and concern.

"Thanks, Mrs. Ahern. We'll take good care of him. And he'll bring home all the information on the games for you," said Danny. But Alicia's face started to dim as she listened, and she turned back to the television.

Danny walked to the door with Michael in tow. He stepped out the door and turned back to the teen. "You've gotta make peace with the team. Whether you go is not my decision."

Michael knew that and nodded.

"We're practicing tomorrow afternoon. If you want to do this, be there."

"I will."

Satisfied, Danny left. Michael stood motionless, thoughts racing through his head. He wanted to go see JP right away, but stopped him-self. He figured that the meeting was better done tomorrow. He had to pick the right time and the right way to mend his relationship with JP. Once that was done, he'd speak with Sam. Everyone else would be cool, he thought.

Michael stepped back in the apartment and took to cleaning up the front room. Alicia eventually got up and walked off to bed. She kissed and hugged Michael when she passed him, not mentioning the basketball conversation.

CHAPTER 31

ONE STEP FORWARD

The Sanchez hamburger stand was moderately busy that afternoon. John Paul walked across the parking lot, his bookbag over his shoulder. Michael looked up from a table he was cleaning and was happy to see his friend. He moved after JP.

"Whass up, JP?"

"What's with you? Been missing school?" JP said with little interest as he kept moving.

"I missed a few days, but I'm back."

JP thought about it for a moment, then shook his head.

"See you, Michael," continuing on.

Michael stopped him. "So, how's the team?"

Sanchez had noticed the two boys speaking, and he closely watched their body language while he went about his work.

"We're going to the Southern Cal competition games," JP said with pride.

Michael said excitedly, "That's cool. So who's playing low post?"

"We're getting someone," JP said.

"Who?"

"I don't know yet," JP answered.

"Well, stop looking. I'm playing," Michael said firmly.

"No, you aren't," JP replied.

"You need me, JP. I'm lucky."

JP looked right at him. "We're a team, and you got no clue what that means."

Michael let himself get sarcastic. "Yeah, I know. You got jerseys."

JP pushed Michael away and turned. "Forget it."

As he started off again, Michael stopped him. "JP, I'm just messin' with you."

Michael stopped. "This is serious, Michael. You do what we do, even painting walls, and stop flappin' that jaw of yours."

"I know. Okay, whatever."

JP did not like Michael's attitude. "Not whatever, it's yeah, I'm with you."

"I am John Paul. I really am. Don't give up on me. Please."

That was the moment, those were the words that convinced John Paul that his friend was serious. He had wanted him to come around, and suddenly it seemed that Michael was ready.

After a moment Michael stuck out his hand with sincerity.

John Paul looked at him for a second, and then their hands connected for the ritual grip of friendship. Still watching, Sanchez smiled.

JP said, "We got practice in an hour."

Michael was anxious. "Yeah, I'll be there. I'll work it out with Sanchez. But I gotta work now. But I'll be there."

JP was on the move and called out, "Later."

Michael gave an affirmative gesture with his clenched fist. He was back.

JP saw that and returned it. As he walked away he said to himself, "Yes, Michael."

Sanchez eyed Michael as the boy entered the kitchen. Sanchez had his portable boombox playing a recording of Cheo's classic "Amor Verdadero," performed by members of the Buena Vista Social Club. Sanchez was doing a few steps as he sang along. With Michael in the room he sang the words in English.

"Guajira, the son is calling you, to dance and enjoy yourself
Come on, my friend have another drink."

Sanchez danced over to the soft drink machine and poured a Coke, which he handed to Michael.

"As your singer, I'll offer you one
Because although it may not interest you
I'm going to tell you my story"

As the song played on Sanchez asked, "So, Michael, how's life, my son?"

Bewildered, Michael said, "I don't know."

Sanchez was still moving to the infectious rhythm and way too happy to be brought down. He began a story, phrased as counterpoint to a wonderful musical solo.

"Amigo, I was just remembering, my brother and me, we would outsmart my father every day. He did not want us playing around the stockyards in Cuernavaca, but we'd sneak down there anyway..." Sanchez laughed as he looked up remembering his brother.

Michael listened and watched as Sanchez put cash and receipts into a large envelope. Sanchez methodically danced to a picture of his father that hung over his desk, pulled it away from the wall and stuck the envelope behind the picture. All this was done to a dance step and the telling of his story.

"The foreman put us to work for a few centavos. We were so proud to have a job and our own money. But later we figured out that our father had set the whole thing up so we'd learn to work. The foreman was his friend. We thought we were so smart. But it was our father who was smart."

Sanchez proudly dusted off his hands and admired the picture.

"Me patrón." It was a portrait of a proud man wearing a caballero's outfit. The black-and-white photo was framed in a classic hand-carved, mahogany frame.

Michael could not help but say, "Mr. Sanchez, that's not a good place to leave money."

"Maybe. But you know, if someone searched that much and found it, they would need it pretty bad, no?"

Michael did not exactly understand what Sanchez meant and said, "Maybe."

Then Sanchez asked, "So, why is life so difficult today?"

"Mr. Sanchez, I got a big problem."

"For such a face you are wearing, it must be big. And what is this problem?"

"I play basketball. My team, they need me. I've gotta stop working because there's this competition in the mountains that's really important and they need me. I really want to go."

"Mi comprendes. So go. When it's all done, I'll still be here. Your job will be too."

Michael was only partially relieved as he said, "Thanks, Mr. Sanchez."

"I'll figure out your pay. Esta bien?"

Michael smiled. "That'd be great. Thanks."

Sanchez understood Michael in a way the boy had never known. He watched as Sanchez scratched out some numbers on a pad. Michael looked out the window and saw Roxanne and her friends. Sanchez caught Michael watching as he counted out the boy's pay. Sanchez handed the cash to Michael.

Sanchez said, "You work hard. This is my pleasure."

"Thanks, Mr. Sanchez."

Michael hesitated; Sanchez knew that something else was on Michael's mind.

Sanchez decided to reach out. "I want to say something, Michael. Going to play basketball with your friends, this is a good thing. That girl out there, no good."

Michael looked outside, a part of him knowing Sanchez was right.

After a moment Sanchez said, "Now, go."

Michael was out the door in a flash. Sanchez watched while starting the CD again.

Roxanne spotted Michael as he crossed the lot in a hurry.

"Hey, Michael. Slow your roll."

He reluctantly stopped. "What, Roxanne?"

Roxanne coyly said, "Ooh. Attitude. RTD are you?" giving him a nasty smile. "Word is you got fame." She waited for a response but he gave her none. "So, whadda you doin' with this Herb job?"

Michael looked directly in her painted eyes. "I don't have time for bullshit, Roxanne. So get on with your skank ass. Bounce."

Roxanne could not believe what she heard.

"What did you say? Fool!"

And Michael did not duck from her reaction. He cut her loose with one phrase. "Kick rocks, loser." He waited a moment, then walked off.

Inside, Sanchez was doing a big-time mambo, loving what he had just seen. He gave Michael an unseen thumbs up and went on about his work, dancing.

Michael was a few minutes early for practice at the playground. Alonzo was in his position just off the top of the key, practicing his shot. Michael watched him for a moment. Alonzo looked pretty con-

fident and that pleased Michael. He snuck up on his friend and surprised him as he stole the bouncing ball out of Alonzo's hands.

Alonzo was really happy to see him. "Michael!"

"Zo! You lookin' good, son. Money shot."

"I'm down with that."

They slapped skins and then started a little scrimmage. Michael
felt really great being back on the court. The other guys joined in as
they arrived for practice, all happy to see Michael on the court. By the
time Kathy and Danny arrived, John Paul, Sam, Alonzo, Anthony, and
Michael were playing the game. They were a team. It was a wonderful sight to behold.

Later that evening Michael arrived home to a red eviction notice on
the door. It said they had three days to leave.

The manager came up behind Michael and said, "Tell your mother, boy. She pays me, or the sheriff will force you out of here."

Michael reached in his pocket and handed him the money he had.
It was $65. "Will this help?" Michael asked.

The manager took it, counted it out loud. Then he looked at
Michael, "Boy, you get me the rest of last month's rent, $350, and I'll
see what I can do. And tell your mother she's lucky you came along."

The manager walked off.

Inside Alicia was drunk. Michael tried to speak with her, but she was
incoherent. He wanted her to know about the eviction notice, and to
help figure out what to do. But he had seen her in this condition
before and knew it would be tomorrow before he could speak with
her. He gave up, knowing he had to do something on his own because
the team was leaving in the morning for the competition.

CHAPTER 32

TWO STEPS BACK

I t was all quiet at the Sanchez hamburger stand. The parking lot was empty. Michael, barely visible in the darkness, approached the kitchen door. He looked around carefully, then reached up over the door lintel feeling for the key. He found it, put the key in the lock, turned it and entered.

Later, Michael sat in the front room of his apartment and stuffed into a black plastic trash bag the few articles of clothing he would take with him. Then he wrote a note.

Mom,

This will take care of the manager.

It's from my job.

Here's the papers on the competition.

Please take care of yourself.

Michael

He placed a stack of bills on top of the note. Next to it, he placed a one-page description of the "2005 Summer Southern Cal Sports Competition."

CHAPTER 33

ACES & 8s

It was the next morning, and Poppi was sitting alone at the kitchen table, playing solitaire. His breakfast dish sat on the table next to the cards complete with the morning's cigarette butts stuck in the remainder of his egg.

Chris entered carrying a brown grocery bag.

Poppi brightened up as he saw his grandson, "Sonny boy!"

"Hey, Poppi. How you doing today?"

Poppi smiled warmly, watching his grandson unload a tub of fresh strawberries, a carton of cream and a carton of cigarettes.

Poppi said, "Better now that you've showed up."

Chris opened the cigarette carton and tossed a pack to Poppi. As Chris put away the food, Poppi reached into the heater closet behind him and pulled out a hidden pint of Jack Daniel's.

"Pass me a glass with some ice, will you, son?"

While Chris reluctantly obliged him, Poppi lit a cigarette.

Chris handed him the glass. "Here you go. You know, Dad, he doesn't. . ."

Poppi stopped him. "Your father needs to mind his business."

Chris picked up Poppi's breakfast dish and cleaned it in the sink. "He worries about you, Poppi."

"I know what that quack sawbones said. At this point, what difference can it make whether I have a drink or not?"

Chris pointed out, "You could fall and break a hip. Anyways, I thought I'd hang here until he gets home, maybe you and me play some poker."

Poppi smiled. "That'd be okay with me. You know, he's up in the mountains with that basketball team. Won't be home for a couple more days."

Chris took a seat, and with a mock serious pose, he said, "Then I guess we're gonna play some real poker."

Poppi nodded and pushed the deck over to him.

Poppi held onto the deck and said, "We miss you around here."

"Me too."

Then Poppi opened a door of thought. "You oughta give us another try."

"I don't think it's my choice," Chris responded.

Poppi let go of the cards. "I wouldn't bet that hand."

Chris took a long look. He knew that his Poppi was a wise old fox worth studying.

Poppi went on. "How you live each day is what counts. That's all your dad wants you to know."

Chris thought about what his grandfather was saying as Poppi raised his glass and asked, "Want to join me?"

"Naw. I'm not doing that anymore. At least, that's my plan right now."

Poppi just looked at him.

Chris continued, "Believe it or not."

Poppi spoke up. "I believe you. You are my grandson. And I think it's a good plan. You don't need this stuff to enjoy yourself."

Chris agreed and grinned. "You're right."

Poppi shifted into the important stuff and said, "Deal."

Chris took the cards and shuffled with confidence. "Five card stud suit you?"

Poppi said, "As long as you don't deal me the dead man's hand."

"No aces and eights today, Poppi."

CHAPTER 34

S tretched between tall pines a banner welcomed participants with the words "2005 Summer Southern Cal Sports Competition." It was stretched above the driveway leading to the Southern California mountain camp. This was the home of the event the boys had worked so hard for. The parking lot was abuzz with activity. Participants twelve to seventeen were lined up to register.

On the playing field, courts, and pool area, athletes practiced while volunteers attached red, white and blue banners, bunting, and pennants to the front of the bleachers and every light standard.

Danny's Explorer and Kathy's Mustang rolled into the parking area. Their callow passengers were taking in the level of the event and the activity. Danny and Kathy found parking spaces toward the lot's end, on the edge of the forest. As the boys got out they were wide-eyed: It was the first time any of them had been in the mountains, away from the city and its sounds and smells.

As Danny and Kathy gathered them together, all heads turned to follow four very perky sixteen-year-old girls as they jogged by. Kathy observed the testosterone levels rising in all of them, including Danny. She elbowed him and brought him back to earth.

He did the same for the boys as he spoke. "Okay, boys, listen up. Kathy and I have to register and get the play schedule. So go check out the campus."

Kathy added, "Good idea to get used to this place before the games start. Oh yeah. Did you decide who is captain?"

Sam spoke first. "John Paul, you know what I'm sayin'."

The boys looked around at each other in agreement.

Alonzo was pleased. "Yo, JP."

JP was proud of the honor, but played it cool in front of his teammates.

"Right. You okay with that, JP?" Kathy asked.

"Yeah."

Kathy nodded, made a note on her clipboard then started off with Danny for the registration tables. The boys moved off.

Four teams, each clad in new uniforms, moved like pros as they practiced on the basketball courts. Kathy and Danny's team, in their neighborhood garb, looked on. They felt intimidated as they noticed the complete picture: the quality of the others' shoes, the practice sweats, the basic look of the players. The boys realized the other players were from the "power" side of the tracks. These were not the kinds of players they were used to seeing.

A practice ball was knocked off the court, and Michael fielded it. A well-groomed fifteen-year-old white player moved toward Michael expecting to receive the ball. Michael held it for a moment, though, just looking at the player.

The player finally asked, "Excuse me—the ball?"

JP turned to Michael.

"Give him the ball."

Michael fired a hard pass. The player looked at him with a "What did I do?" expression.

JP offered, "Sorry, dude."

The player was cool. "No problem." He returned to the court, and their practice resumed.

Anthony reverted to s'language. "Ese, them boyz is good."

Alonzo observed, "And look how many of them."

Then Sam weighed in. "They'll wear us out, know what I'm sayin'?"

JP grabbed his teammates' attention with, "It don't matter how many. We play ball in quarters, four quarters."

Sam got it. He nodded. So did Anthony. For the moment, at least, it seemed to assuage their concern. JP looked at Michael, who was walking away.

"Later, dudes." He walked off after Michael.

When he caught up to him JP said, "What's with you?"

"Nothin'. Just didn't like the way the three-ten preppie looks.

"You had his ball!"

Michael looked the other way. He knew he could not justify his attitude.

JP jumped in his face. "Is this what it's always gonna be? You don't like his face, you don't got time, school's for fools?"

Michael admitted, "Okay, I got pissed looking at their cool threads and their cool shoes. Bet their daddies got the duckets.

JP asked, "So?"

"It ain't fair."

JP was angry. "I'm tired of you trashin' everything. Lose it here and you screw all of us."

Michael turned away again. After a moment John Paul walked off. As he went in search of the others, he thought about Michael, the odd man out. They could not be a team without him. But could they be a team with him?

And Michael moved in the other direction saying to himself, "Idiot." He was pissed that he had let that angry thing come up and grab him.

Michael walked on, passing many teens in practice. He passed the track and field area, where a team was running an obstacle course. He saw teammates encouraging each other through the tough obstacles and hurdles. A moment later, he passed a group of girls wearing their team bathing suits. His eyes met Alyssum's. She separated from her friends and stopped, surprised.

Brightly she said, "Hi."

"Hi."

"So, you made it."

"I missed a few days, but I'm back."

She could sense his distraction. "You okay?"

"Yeah. Lotta stuff goin' on."

Alyssum felt pressure from her friends, who were waiting. Before walking on she said, "Maybe we'll see each other later?"

Rather than committing to anything, Michael simply said, "Good luck."

Disappointed she responded. "You too."

He watched as she walked off.

Michael spent the next few hours alone, perched on top of a boulder that gave him a view to a meadow west of the camp. The Sanchez matter was weighing heavily on him, along with his concern for his mother. The new experience of this environment distracted him from those thoughts, and he relaxed in the sun. He watched ground squirrels busily gathering; a red-tail hawk surveyed the meadow, then swooped down on its prey; a coyote, with an injured front leg, moved swiftly looking for a meal despite its disability. It struck him that these animals were handling life on their own, and that gave him comfort. He realized lots of creatures are simply trying to survive.

Mid-afternoon, he set out to find his teammates.

It was later in the afternoon. At the top of a rise sat the last of several identical cabins. The boys were unloading the Explorer and the Mustang.

The cabin was very basic. Rows of bunks, overhead lights, windows all around and no bathroom, this was a dorm setup. The boys were unrolling bedrolls on the bunks.

Danny stepped in. "Okay, guys, I got some work details. Michael and John Paul, you two start cleaning. Anthony and Sam, start gathering firewood. Alonzo, see if you can find water."

Alonzo piped up, "Excuse me. Where's the bathroom?"

Danny pointed, "Across the bridge, the first building."

Anthony looked, not believing what he just heard. "But what do I...I mean, at night, in the dark?"

Sam answered him humorously. "Be careful where you puttin' them big feet. There's bears in dem woods, you know what I'm sayin'."

There were nervous chuckles from the others.

"Where we gonna eat?" asked Alonzo.

"Out there." Kathy was pointing toward the fire pit beyond the front steps.

They looked, and then looked back at her not understanding.

She added, "We're camping."

Alonzo had to ask, "But who's going to cook?"

They all looked at Kathy.

Her response was immediate. "Don't be looking at me."

Danny took over, "We'll take turns. Be good for you to learn how to take care of yourselves. Now get started with your duties. It'll be dark soon."

The boys slowly began moving. Danny added, "If you don't get the lead out of your asses, you'll be going to bed hungry and cold. Now, move!"

The boys jumped into gear and started off.

Danny and Kathy headed outside to finish unloading the cars.

It was one of those pitch-black nights only seen when far enough away from the reflected glow of a city's lights. The moon had not risen yet and the sky was filled with stars. Their dinner was done, kerosene lamps burned with a warm but dim light that embellished the glow from the remaining embers in the fire pit. Danny was directing the group as they cleaned up, putting paper plates in trash bags. They finished and Kathy had a bag of marshmallows and a selection of honed branches ready to skewer them for roasting over the fire.

She and Danny demonstrated the fine art of preparing this fun, campsite dessert. At first try, the boys lost a few to the fire, but in the end they succeeded in stuffing their bellies. The day had been filled with lots of new experiences and a new world of memories was to be carried with them through life.

Kathy got their attention standing by the fire. "It's time to get our heads into tomorrow's game."

Kathy picked up a piece of wood as if to stoke the fire, but she moved in the other direction.

Anthony commented with concern, "They're gonna kick our butts."

Kathy blew out one of the oil lamps. It became noticeably darker.

Sam followed up on Anthony's concern. "Or run our butts off. How many boyz on those teams? Know what I'm sayin'?"

Danny offered, "Only five play at a time."

Kathy blew out the other lamp. It was now dark.

Alonzo began squirming. "Hey, what's with the torches?"

Kathy made no comment and Danny played along, though not certain what she was up to. It became really quiet. Kathy tossed the wood she was carrying at a bush just beyond the cabin. It landed with a loud noise, scaring the boys.

Their comments were loaded with wide-eyed fright. "Shit. Damn. Who's that?"

Kathy moved by the fire pit. "Scared? You never know what might crawl up behind you, Alonzo."

Alonzo jumped up. The others could barely make out silhouettes of each other. He stepped on Anthony, who hissed, "Ese. Watch the feet!"

Alonzo pleaded, "Please, no witch stories." He tried to walk but could not see where he was putting his feet. Then he tripped over Sam and fell.

As Alonzo untangled himself and got up, Sam reacted. "Damn, Lonzo. Sit your butt down, you know what I'm sayin'?"

Danny spoke up. "Easy, High-top."

Once things settled down, Kathy began. "If you learn to live in the darkness, you won't be afraid of it. Learn to live with fear you'll begin to understand it. John Paul, where's the door to the cabin?"

He looked around barely able to see the door. He pointed, hesitantly adding, "Over there."

Kathy went on. "Walk to it and open it, please."

John Paul questioned her. "Me? In the dark?"

"Yes, you. In the dark."

John Paul got up, fumbled, moved cautiously, not without a few snickers from the boys, but eventually opened the door.

"Good. You overcame your fear." Kathy struck a match and re-lit a lamp. She continued. "You just needed to trust yourself, think about each step, not take anything for granted."

JP was getting the concept. It actually felt really cool to him that he had overcome the darkness. "Cool. I get the idea. I can see in the dark." At that moment he tripped over Sam's purposefully placed foot.

The boys laughed and JP teased back, "Oh, I didn't see you takin' no steps in the dark."

Kathy interrupted the boys. "Okay, JP. So what's my point?" she asked.

JP did not hesitate to answer. "Get on top of the fear so it doesn't get on top of you. Like it got on these fools."

JP got some jeers from his buddies as he took a seat.

Kathy lit the other lamp, then stoked the fire as she continued. "Don't let all the noise, the people, cheerleaders, pressure, all that other stuff, don't let them distract you. Keep your head in the game. Be a team. You know each other well. You trust each other."

Danny jumped in. "And don't get intimidated by fancy uniforms. You know, in my business, every time I come up against some tough guy, even if I'm twice his size, my asshole puckers."

Kathy grinned, adding, "You do that too?"

Sam and Anthony laughed.

Danny went on. "It's okay to be scared. The other guy is just as scared. And play tough off the boards. Now, let's gather close together."

The boys moved in closer, not knowing what for.

Danny continued. "Gather hands in a circle. We need to say a little prayer."

They formed a circle and following Danny's and Kathy's lead, gathered hands. Michael was the last one to join and fell in line next to John Paul.

Danny began a prayer. "We've pulled together to get here with some real help from above, and we thank you for that blessing. Tomorrow the five of you are going out on those courts. You all know this wouldn't have happened without Art's believing in you. So I want each of you to say a prayer and thank him."

Sam dropped his head in prayer, as did JP and Michael. Anthony put his hands together in prayer just over his chest, his eyes closed. Alonzo did also, but kept his eyes open. They all prayed for Art silently. They prayed for their families. And they prayed to win.

Alonzo looked at each of his buddies as he prayed, wanting them to know what it meant to him to be in the game with them. They were all so cool. High-top could defend like Shaq, Michael had the moves and could shoot from outside or take it downtown, Tone was shifty and really hard to guard. He did the best layup because he knew how to drive inside through the traffic. And JP was the anchor for Alonzo. He did everything really well. JP was steady, never lost his cool. Of all of them, if he could, Alonzo wanted to be like JP.

Danny prayed. He thought about Art and wished he had helped

with the boys while his good friend was coaching them. Then he thought about Chris. Why couldn't this kind of thing have ever happened with his own son? He had missed these kinds of days with his boy. Somehow he had to invent the new days, the new experiences that would fill the void that existed.

And Kathy meditated in the few moments of silence. She wanted a calm to take over. It was through composure that she would focus all her energy into this moment in time. She had learned to do that in her winning days at UCLA. The boys would need that calm strength. They would need to look into her eyes as she had done with her coaches so many times.

A few moments passed and Danny said, "Amen."

The prayer complete, Kathy spoke up. "Let's wrap up. Sunrise is coming soon."

The boys moved toward the cabin.

The boys were settled in their bunks. The lights were off. Danny was standing at the doorway about to go outside to the fire.

JP asked, "What time's the first game?"

Danny replied, "Eight o'clock."

Michael said, "That early?"

Sam chimed in. "Yeah, fool. You better be ready. You know what I'm sayin'."

Michael made a comment under his breath that Sam heard. "You better be ready."

Danny stepped in. "You two, zip it up."

They all mumbled "good night" as Danny closed the door. The boys were all spending their first night away from home and their mothers. John Paul was lying on his back looking through the window. Light washed over his excited face from the huge rising moon. Sam, Alonzo, Anthony and Michael were doing the same, looking up at the intense light.

Michael's face, unlike the others, showed fright. His mind was not here. It was back at Sanchez's. Certainly the man had discovered the missing money. Michael kept seeing his face, knowing that even though he intended to return the money to him, it was theft. He had taken something without permission. Sanchez had said that if some-one took it, he must need it pretty bad. Michael was trying desperately to find a way to justify what he had done to help his mother. The truth was in front of him. He kept seeing Sanchez, dancing to the music, putting the money away.

He was looking at the full moon, so bright the sky around it was blue. The moon had a face that evening, and it reminded Michael of Art. Then Michael heard his voice. "Wanna play one on one, Michael? You can play pickup ball any time. Wanna be in this posse, do it my way." Michael kept staring at the moon long after the others were asleep. He fell asleep sometime after remembering the story Art asked him about. "Shake the dirt off your shoulders, Michael. Remember the donkey that wouldn't give up when the farmer couldn't get him out of the well. Remember the story?"

Kathy and Danny spent a few moments by the fire. They wondered how it would go the next day. All the doubt came out. Was it right to bring the boys up here to face this kind of challenge? Were they ready? If any of them got injured, the team was in trouble. Finally they agreed—this was a great experience regardless of all the unknowns.

Danny had wanted to talk to her about how much he respected what she was doing for the boys, and now he had his opportunity.

"Coach, I gotta say something right now, and there couldn't be a better time for me to do it."

Kathy had no idea what this was about. She leaned back, folding her arms saying, "I'm all ears."

He continued. "When you asked me to help you paint the rec room, I thought you were nuts. When you suggested we coach the boys, well, I was certain you weren't wrapped too tight. But, little by little, you have taken these boys from scrappy playground urchins to disciplined members of a team. That's like, unthinkable. You are really amazing. I'm proud to say, they are a team. I just wish Art were here."

"Thanks, Danny. I really appreciate you saying that," she said with a smile.

However, on this evening Danny mostly wanted to thank her for something else.

"The truth is, I feel very lucky you asked me to help out. I mean, you're the one with the game plan, the experience. I'm just happy to be a part of this and carry the water." He paused for a moment, then continued with, "Kathy Montalvo, I think you're pretty damn special."

Danny's words blew her away to the point that it took a few moments before she could respond. And she too wanted Danny to know how great it was to have him in this with her. For certainly she knew she could never have pulled it off without him. But then that was the essence they were both trying to bring into the boys' lives: teamwork.

They said their goodnights and doused the fire. As Danny took one of the lanterns, he turned to her. "You still owe me a dance."

"And you shall have it," Kathy replied. She took the other lantern and went to her tent, pitched next to her car. She stopped before entering it and looked up at the incredible moon, now offering a warm light that filled the mountain valley. She gazed at it for a few moments. It seemed so much closer than it did in the city.

Inside her tent, by dim lantern light, she quietly chanted her evening Gongyo. She would invoke the power of the universe to give her boys focus and strength of purpose.

CHAPTER 35

T
he basketball crossed a blue sky and swished through the net as if it had eyes. An official blew his whistle.

The Hawks were playing the Saints in both teams' first games. Michael and the Saints' #17 were picking themselves up from a fall. The referee called the foul on Michael, and his first instinct was to argue. Fearing how far he might take it, JP held Michael back and argued the call for him.

JP was pointing at #17. "He ran over my man!"

Michael was surprised by John Paul's intervention. He held back, enjoying the support. On the sidelines, Danny and Kathy paced nervously. She waved JP away from the confrontation.

Kathy yelled, "Get some eyes, Stripes."

The ref called to the bench. "Foul. Number twenty-six, Hawks."

The ref took a position at the key as the teams lined up for a free throw. He tossed the ball to #17 as Kathy made the timeout sign to JP. He in turn called for it.

The ref gestured acknowledgment, blowing his whistle and pointing to the timekeeper. The clock had stopped with eight seconds left. The score: Saints 37, Hawks 36.

The Hawks huddled up on the sidelines with Kathy in the center, down on one knee. Danny stood right behind her. Kathy looked up at the five boys who were fanned out around her in a half circle.

Danny said, "Cut off the lanes, guys."

Kathy agreed. "He's right. You're letting 'em penetrate.

"Michael, stick with your man just like you've been doing. You're making him chuck it from outside. That's good."

That made Michael feel good. He was really trying to be a team player, finding his way to a balance between his playground style and this team sport.

Kathy continued, "After this guy's second shot, get back on defense. Don't let them run you off the boards."

Danny added, "Rebound."

Kathy went on. "John Paul, don't forget—be patient, work for the good shot. Now, go in there and win your first game."

They clapped and broke the huddle.

Play resumed as #17 took his two shots, making the first, missing the second. The ball went in play; the action was intense. The score stayed within one point as the clock ran down, the lead changing sides several times. By the time fifteen seconds were left, the Hawks were again down by one point.

Kathy motioned to JP for a timeout. Three more seconds and the clock stopped.

At the bench, Kathy looked up at the boys' faces. These teens had never been in a more intense situation, nor felt such pressure. She had been where they stood many a time. She remembered being so intensely tied into the floor action that she needed her coach to tell her what to do. Now the tables were turned, and all eyes were on her. She had to guide those five boys to a victory to make good on the entire season of practice that brought them here.

Kathy decided to compliment them first. "In case you haven't realized it yet, you are good enough to be here. And you're better than those guys."

It pleased them to hear that; all eyes stayed right on her, waiting for words of wisdom. What were they to do with the twelve seconds left in the game?

She continued. "Okay, twelve seconds left. Work for the last shot, so there's no surprises we'll give'em what they expect. Anthony, go high, receive the pass, drive to the top of the key. Use up three seconds. Pass to JP moving across the top of the key. Watch the clock, it'll be inside ten. JP, pass to Michael low. This is what they'll expect. As the defense drops to cover Michael, kick it off to Alonzo."

Alonzo could not believe his name was in for the final and deciding shot of the game. Kathy pointed to him. "You, set and shoot."

Alonzo looked uncertain.

Kathy continued, "This is your shot, Alonzo. This is the one you've been practicing for."

Danny looked into his eyes. "You can do this."

Alonzo felt a swell of determination, and his confidence rose.

Alonzo straightened up. "Yo. Let's roll."

They clapped and broke the huddle.

As they returned to the court, Alonzo looked up to the scoreboard. Saints 49, Hawks 48. The time remaining: twelve seconds. That felt like destiny to Alonzo. So many times had he watched NBA games and cheered as his hero, Shaq, had scored a clutch shot. This was Alonzo's moment. He was ready.

Michael passed him and said, "Zo. It's all yours bro."

JP followed and said, "Your money shot, Lonzo."

It was indeed. For the past three months Alonzo had made that shot so many times, he went to sleep thinking about the ball dropping through the net. But his hands had never felt wet as they did right now. And he did not know if he could hold onto the ball.

The official blew the whistle and play resumed. Anthony took the inbound pass from Sam and drove in. Alonzo moved into his position. Eleven seconds, ten, and Anthony passed to JP, who made a move toward the basket and drew his man and another defender closer to him. He passed to Michael, who drew the defense toward him.

It was perfect. Kathy looked over to the clock. It was running down just as she had planned: seven seconds, six, five.

Michael made the move for the fake shot and kept the defenders on him. Then he passed off to Alonzo, who by now was totally alone. Zo received the perfect pass and set.

The defense was caught totally off-guard. Alonzo knew this was his moment. The backcourt Saints rushed toward him. The clock was ticking three seconds, two. Alonzo let the ball go. It spun in its arc of destiny.

All the faces on the court and the sidelines watched the ball. The clock passed one and the buzzer sounded. Alonzo watched, his hand still in the air from releasing the shot.

The ball hit the hoop, did a partial circle and then dropped through for two points.

Alonzo pointed his index finger straight down. His dream had just come true. He won the game. He took the clincher shot. Kathy had designed it for him. All the guys he loved had supported him in this. How perfect a moment was this?

Alonzo did not hear the whistle blow. Everything went into slow motion for him as the Hawks, his buddies, his crew, all jumped for joy. High-fives around, they all slapped skins with Lonzo.

Then the boys moved toward the jubilant Kathy and the amazed Danny. After the boys let out a few triumphant screams, Kathy and Danny settled them down.

Alonzo was Mr. Cool. "Yeah."

JP high-fived Alonzo again, but Michael went a little further and hugged him.

"Yeah, I'm down with this scene," John Paul said.

Danny hugged Alonzo. "That's aces! Alonzo, ever felt better?"

Alonzo replied. "Yo. It come off my fingertips, and I knew, all the way."

Sam stepped over. "Yo, Zo. You know what I'm saying." And they high-fived.

Kathy hugged Alonzo. "Beautiful shot."

Anthony added, "Yo. We'll beat all these fools."

Danny replied, "Easy, Tone. You got a long distance to run and the fat lady ain't sung, yet."

Anthony asked, "What fat lady?"

Danny replied, "Never mind. Just listen up."

Kathy said, "We've got about four hours till your next game, so let's move around, get some food, relax."

Alonzo, still being cool, said, "I'm struttin' my stuff."

Danny laughed. "Damn right you are."

The Hawks and their coaches moved off, the sunshine never feeling so bright, the air so good. They were walking tall. The world was theirs to take.

CHAPTER 36

The Hawks moved around the campus. They were walking tall, especially when a few spectators commented to them about their victory. Waiting till their next game, they watched track events, pole-vaulting, long-jumping and other field competitions. Girls' water polo was their favorite.

Michael's eyes meet Alyssum's just as she went in for a series of plays. She outreached her opponent and hit a shot that scored. Michael yelled out, "Yo, Alyssum!" The other guys picked up on it and also yelled out, "Yo, Alyssum!" Though a little embarrassed, she loved the attention.

It was late afternoon. The sun was making play difficult on the home end of the court. Michael was reaching to the sky to block a shot. He was bumped by his man and the ball got past him finding the basket.

The referee called the foul on Michael. Kathy was getting frustrated. It was not a good game for the Hawks. The Regents were dominating them.

She yelled, "You need glasses, stripes!"

There was less than two minutes left on the game clock, the score was Regents 53, Hawks 31. Play resumed with JP bringing the ball down the court. He passed off to Tone, who did one of his signature drives but ran into a wall of defenders. He spun and passed to Michael, who began a drive from the top of the key. He was totally ignoring two open men, JP and High-top.

Kathy and Danny were yelling at him, "Pass!"

Danny added, "Find your man. Michael! Set up a shot!"

Instead of passing it off, Michael tried the layup. He missed. The Regents got the rebound and beat the Hawks to the other end for an easy layup.

Kathy was doing her best not to lose it. She conferred with Danny as the game continued downhill.

Kathy admitted, "Suppose it wasn't so good to win the first one."

Danny responded, "I don't know. We'd never get them to try again if they hadn't tasted victory."

The game came to a close with the Regents winning 67 to 41.

The Hawks, spiritless, hung their heads as they walked off the court.

The team was gathered around the fire pit in front of their cabin. It was after dinner and all was quiet. Kathy and Danny looked at the boys. It was time for a reflective team meeting.

"Anybody want to tell me what went wrong?" Kathy asked.

Sam did not hesitate. "They kicked our butts, you know what I'm sayin'."

Alonzo countered. "We know that, fool." The others remained quiet.

JP stepped in to the conversation. "We didn't play like a team. We were fools."

Kathy seized on his words. "You weren't the same team that won this morning. And the really sad thing is the Regents are an easier team than the Saints. You coulda beat 'em. It was embarrassing. You got frustrated. Things started to fall apart. Instead of going for what we practiced, you went back to a street game. They picked you guys apart. You looked like the Lakers falling to the Pistons when team-work took down the mighty champions."

She meant it and they knew it.

Danny added, "How bad do you want it? Think about it. All the practice, what was it for?"

There was a lot of thought going on in that moment. Then Michael spoke up. "How we gonna play those bitches again?"

Danny answered. "In the first three days, you play six games. The top four teams advance to the medal round. The top two play for gold, three and four play for bronze."

They began to perk up at the realization that all was not lost.

Danny continued. "We could play them again, if you fools win enough games to advance."

A few more moments passed.

John Paul spoke out. "Yeah, we are a team. We wouldn't be here if we weren't."

Sam got into it. "Yeah, and Art got us started, you know what I'm sayin'."

"Yeah," JP said with conviction. It was building inside him. He got up nodding his head. Alonzo joined him with a fist-bang vote of confidence.

Alonzo said, "Yeah, we can beat those bitches."

The boys agreed and they slapped skins.

In unison they said, "Yeah!"

Michael moved over to John Paul. "For Art!"

JP agreed. "For Art!"

Kathy and Danny nodded in agreement.

CHAPTER 37

A NEW LIFE

The new day brought a new life to the Hawks. Sam was solid on defense, Michael passed to JP and Anthony instead of trying to do it alone. Alonzo was solid. Kathy and Danny high-fived the boys at the end of each quarter, and at the end of the morning game their team defeated the opponent.

In the afternoon game, the Hawks were the same well-oiled machine operating with precision. Alonzo made his free throws, and Anthony made a beautiful layup after receiving a pass from John Paul. The scoreboard showed another Hawk victory.

The boys were strong, confident, and quick, but they did not go through the victory celebration with each win. They high-fived each other, giving deserved compliments. However, there was no cocky display. They just moved on like pros to the next team.

In the next game, Michael continued to amaze them all. And when he spotted Alyssum watching, he was even stronger. She gave him a big thumbs up. In his next play Michael was knocked down and fouled. No temper flare-up, he got up, gathered himself, and made his free throws. Danny gave him a high-five. Another series of rapid layups and twenty-footers, and the scoreboard showed another Hawks victory. However, this time Kathy and Danny let loose with screams.

Kathy announced, "You guys are in the medal round."

Playfully coming up from behind her, Danny picked Kathy up and spun her around in excitement. It was a little awkward as he put her down.

Danny looked embarrassed and offered, "Wow, I just got so excited. But I know, it's a sexist thing. Should'a asked first, right?"

Kathy was smiling, still very excited.

A slow grin came over Danny's face. She threw her arms around his neck and planted a kiss on him that left him speechless. Alonzo saw it and did a catcall.

A few feet away Michael and JP had clasped hands in a shake.

"I been thinking about a lot of stuff. Thanks for not giving up on me," Michael said.

"What'a you talking trash for? You're part of us."

Michael continued, "I won't ever forget this, JP. Just want you to know."

The two boys hugged, and the Hawks moved off across the field, arm in arm. Kathy and Danny brought up the rear like proud parents.

Kathy was amazed at the sight. "Did you see John Paul and Michael?"

Danny responded, "Did I see them? Are you nuts? Have you seen 'em all? What a change."

"The best? From here on out, it doesn't matter what happens."

Danny cocked his head. "Yeah, it does. They gotta win one more, and they'll go home with a medal."

Kathy put out her palm. "Now that would be hot."

Danny gave her five and they continued on following their amazed, and amazing, boys.

This was the last night of the camp. All the competitors were gathered around the main campfire for an evening of entertainment. A guitarist/singer was performing. Just beyond the fire pit was a large barbecue dinner spread covering the tables. Kids lined up to get their chow.

Michael was a few yards away in a conversation on a pay phone with his mom.

"So, things are cool with the manager?"

Alicia told him that everything was okay. She told him how nice it was that his boss helped them out.

Michael avoided that point and asked if she was okay. Alicia proudly told him she had not had a drink since he left. That made Michael smile. Then she told him she had cleaned the apartment.

Indeed, Alicia had done a marathon cleanup. It was triggered when the manager complimented her, and told her she was a lucky woman to have a son like Michael. She had looked at herself in the mirror moments later and saw what she had become. Suddenly she realized that she had to find a way to thank her son for keeping things going when she had failed. Paying him recognition for being an adult when he should really still be a kid was now her objective. And it started with the apartment. She wanted him to come back to a clean home, one that showed she cared.

Michael was really surprised when she told him what she had done. But it was her tone, more than the words, that convinced him she really had done a cleanup. Then he said, "You really did? Mom, that's great."

"I really did. I'm going to make some changes. And I'm going back to AA, Michael. I promise you."

Michael knew about that. He had been through other attempts at her sobering up. But it was encouraging to hear her. He was afraid to ask questions or comment for fear of jinxing things.

After a long pause, Alicia asked how his team was doing.

Michael responded excitedly, "We're doing really good. We made the finals."

She told him how proud of him she was. "I wish I could see you."

With real hope, he said, "Next year, okay?"

She said, "Okay."

He told her he had to go and she asked when he was coming home.

"We'll be back tomorrow afternoon. I'll see you tomorrow night."

She told him she'd have dinner ready for him. And then she added, "I love you, Michael."

Michael choked a little and said, "I love you too, Mom." And he added, "You can do it."

"I'm really trying, sweetie."

He slowly hung up the phone. As he turned, Alyssum was waiting.

Politely she asked, "Your girlfriend?"

"No. Checkin' in with my mom."

Alyssum was relieved, and she smiled. "I just did that too. By the way, congratulations."

"Thanks. You saw the game?"

"Yeah, awesome," she added.

"It was pretty cool. So are you. I saw you playing water polo."

"We didn't make the finals." She scrunched her face, showing disappointment, but to Michael she still looked cute.

Michael wished he could do more than say, "Sorry."

"It's okay. Don't worry about it."

"You guys really looked good," he said emphatically.

That made her smile again, and then she asked, "You gonna eat?"

He looked toward the food table. "Yeah, that's cool. You?"

She nodded and they walked to the table.

Michael and Alyssum ate, talked with John Paul, Sam, Alonzo and Anthony, listened to the singer, laughed and played around. The other boys hooked up with some of the girls from Alyssum's team. But through it all, Michael's thoughts drifted back to Sanchez. It could have been a perfect week, but he had a major storm cloud waiting for his return. All this excitement here was going to be overshadowed.

As the night progressed, dancing began. Danny and Kathy took to the dance floor, which got a lot of laughs from the boys. Michael and Alyssum watched as the others danced, but he never offered to join in.

Alyssum could read the trouble in Michael's eyes. So she was not surprised when he said, "I've gotta split."

"Walk me to my cabin?" she asked.

Michael agreed and they left the party.

When Michael and Alyssum approached her cabin she asked, "Wanna talk about what's wrong?"

"Nothing I want to talk about. Just stuff. Trouble."

She reached to his hand, but he did not want the contact and kept to himself.

She sweetly inquired, "You wanna talk? Maybe I can help just listening."

Michael got an edge in his voice. "No! I don't want to talk. It's stuff I gotta work out."

Alyssum gave up. Whatever it was, she realized he was not about to lay it open to her. "Okay, Michael."

Alyssum stepped toward the cabin door.

Michael softened his attitude. "I'll see you tomorrow."

She turned and smiled. "Okay. I hope you have a good sleep, and good luck tomorrow."

"Thanks." He watched as she entered the cabin. After she was safely inside, he walked away.

CHAPTER 38

DEATH GIVES LIFE

The party was over and the campus was getting quiet. The teams had returned to their cabins, finalists thinking about tomorrow, the others next year.

Danny was leaning against the cabin railing looking up at the stars when Michael approached him.

Danny looked at him. "Big day tomorrow. You nervous?"

Michael quickly went for the positive. "No." But just as quickly, he turned honest. "Well, yes."

Danny appreciated the turn to honesty but wanted to find a way to defuse the anxiety. He looked back out at the night.

Michael picked up the conversation, and it became obvious to Danny that he needed to connect. "Can I ask you something?" Michael said.

"Sure."

Michael shifted his position and then spoke, "This guy said this like weird thing. 'That which dies is born'? What's that mean?"

Danny grinned. "Chris is trying to figure that out."

"Dying?" Michael asked with surprise.

"No. Growing up. Shedding one stage of life for the next."

"What does that have to do with dying?"

This was an important question. It was one of those teen adult moments when Danny knew that the answer might impact the boy. At the very least Danny wanted Michael to understand.

Danny pointed to the horizon. "See those trees? They all come from seeds. The seeds come from other trees. But the seeds have to die and fall off the living tree before they begin again. That's life, one thing gives way the other."

Michael was staring at him, not the trees. It looked to Danny as if Michael did not know what to think after that explanation.

Danny dug a little further. "It's like this: You're about to leave all the kid stuff behind. Becoming a man isn't easy, Michael, saying good-bye to what you know is scary. It's the darkness thing. You got to trust in life, and mostly yourself."

Danny was trying to read Michael's face. Was he getting to him? It was too dark, and he really could not tell. So Danny kept the roll going. "You've got to know that way down inside of you, there's a little voice that speaks up. And you are the only one that can hear that voice. It's inside you trying to be heard because you're wanting to be a man. But being a man is not about what you look like, or what kind of shoes you wear on the court, or when you get a little older, what kind of car you drive or how much money you have in your pocket. It's really about trust. You trust yourself and others trust you. To get there, you have to let the kid die away so the man can grow. Men stand up to whatever life throws at them."

Michael's big eyes were studying Danny. Danny studied him back.

Danny went on. "You've got a lot of responsibility, don't you?"

"I just do what I got to."

Danny asked, "How long you worked for Sanchez?"

Michael was uncomfortable. "Why?"

"Just wondering how long you've helped your mom."

Michael was defensive as he answered, "She doesn't need my help. You talkin' about the manager thing at the apartment?"

Danny nodded.

"It's taken care of."

Danny offered, "Well, I've been concerned. This competition is tough enough without having you worried about other stuff."

Danny looked back to the night. "There are times when all the pressure becomes this big weight on your head. Can you imagine a bowling ball, what it would take to chuck it all the way to the basket?"

They chuckled at the thought. At that moment John Paul walked up.

Danny looked over to him. "JP. Ready for the big day?"

JP thought about it for a second, and, with conviction, answered, "Yes, I am. And I think we are."

Danny nodded. "I do too."

He put out his hand, and he and JP did the shake thing, followed by Michael.

Danny turned back to the sky.

"Nothing like the sky up here. Guys, I'm taking a walk. Get some sleep, will you?"

Danny patted them on the backs as he left.

The boys watched him walk off and then gazed at the sky.

JP spoke first. "Wanna hear something weird?"

Michael looked at him. John Paul was still looking at the sky.

John Paul continued. "I thought I heard Art laughing today, when we won."

Michael was surprised at first but added, "I thought I heard him talking to me too."

John Paul turned to him. "Really?"

"Yeah. I thought it was just my memory, but now I'm not so sure."

Michael took a second and then continued, "I was mad at Art, last time I saw him, wishing he'd never come back."

John Paul put his hand on Michael's shoulder. "He's here. Somehow. He's here."

They looked at each other, knowing that it was true.

CHAPTER 39

THE GAME

The Regents were a great team. But on this day the Hawks were at least as good. It was a tough game. The score was close from the start; these guys were running each others' legs off. The teams were never more than five points apart. For coaches and fans, it was nail-biting time. In rebounds, free throws, three-point shots, and from downtown, these teams were neck and neck.

In the midst of the action, without Danny realizing it, Poppi and Chris had arrived at the campus and found seats to watch the action. Alyssum and her friends had formed their own cheerleading squad. As a surprise yet to be seen, Sanchez had found his way to the campus and sat in the upper corner of the bleachers under the shade of a large straw hat. He was seated next to a man who was a Regents fan.

Long before all this energy exploded, Kathy and Danny had taken the boys to the courts. They got up at first light to prepare for their chance, their day of fame. A month ago rising with the sun would have been met by a lot of complaints. But today, whatever the coaches said was a go.

It was a little foggy that morning so the air was heavy, in a good way. As they descended the hill from their cabin, Kathy told the boys she wanted them to walk the court on which they would be playing this crucial game. It was a different court than they had played the other games on. This one was used for the championship games. It had double-deck bleachers running lengthwise on both sides.

What made Kathy nervous was that the court also doubled as the volleyball court. That meant the floor lines were potentially confusing. So she walked them to the out-of-bounds lines, the ten-second line, to the top of the key, then over to where they had placed the scorer's table. She had them look at the scoreboards and the clock. She had them look for any surface imperfections.

Kathy walked over to their bench and had them stand in the middle of the floor and look at her.

Kathy said, "See where I am? See what's behind me?"

They were looking at empty bleachers. A moment passed and Alonzo pointed toward the top of the bleachers.

"The mountains. You're standing on their side." Alonzo said this proudly, quite pleased to have figured out what she was looking for.

"Yo, Einstein." Sam said this and then high-fived Alonzo.

"Right, Lonzo." Kathy nodded her head and pointed at him. "Way to think. This place is going to be a mob of people. It's going to be noisy, and you're going to have a hard time knowing where to be looking for Danny and me. Remember those mountains. No one's going to hide them from you."

The pre-game thinking and conditioning had paid off. The Hawks played like it was their home court. And now here they were with seven seconds left on the play clock and the score was Hawks 43, Regents 45. The Regents were ten deep on their bench. To the Hawks, bench depth was a concept they could not imagine.

John Paul received the ball on an inbound pass from Anthony and drove in, passing off to Michael. He made a great move on his defender and went in for a layup. As he went up, the defender fouled him but the shot was good. The game was tied with no time left on the clock.

The man next to Sanchez looked as if he were about to have a nervous breakdown. Sanchez asked the man to explain why the game was still being played with zero seconds left.

The man explained that the Hawks had a chance to score the winning point from the free-throw line. If the shooter missed, then the game would go into overtime. The man was sure the Regents would win, if they could get into extra minutes. When the Regents fan looked back to the game, Sanchez looked up, said a quick prayer, then made the sign of the cross.

On the sidelines Kathy and Danny could barely stand the pressure. Danny looked to the sky and said, "Just one more point, Lord. Please."

Without looking at him, Kathy said, "You better ask him again."

"What?" Danny asked.

She gestured to the heavens. "Your prayer. Make sure he heard you."

Danny looked up again. "Whatever you want, Lord."

Kathy looked at him. "I'm going to hold you to that one."

The teams were formed up around the key. The ref shot the ball to Michael. He looked up at the basket. It was a million miles away. He dribbled the ball. A bead of sweat dropped off his nose.

John Paul was hunched over, watching with great intensity.

He called out to Michael, "Easy, bro. You're the money."

Poppy and Chris watched as Michael took another couple of bounces, then looked up at the basket. It still seemed a long way out there. And suddenly his palms felt sticky.

"Dust the dirt off your shoulders." It was Art again. Michael looked at the sidelines. He knew he had heard Art's voice. His eyes searched. He saw Alyssum watching him with a very intense expression, her hands raised to her mouth in prayer. Then he spotted Danny and Kathy, who seemed to be moving in slow motion.

Alonzo got his attention from the line. "Yo, bro. You got this one."

Kathy and Danny clapped from the sidelines. Michael trained in on Kathy. She was sending him every measure of energy she had. They were eye to eye with twenty-five feet between them. The distance had evaporated, however. No one else was on the court for that split second. And in that moment, no doubt, Kathy was offering a Nam-Myoho-Renge-Kyo along with channeling every degree of energy she could to Michael.

Michael looked at Danny and could hear him saying the words he had said last night, "It's like chucking a bowling ball." He looked up at the basket again as he bounced the ball. It did seem heavier so he looked down at the court.

Sam, hands on his knees, had both his fingers crossed and called out, "Yo. Michael. You the man, know what I'm sayin."

With reassuring confidence Anthony said, "Ese, it's got eyes."

Michael focused on the hoop. Suddenly all the sounds went away. He could hear only his heart pumping. He set. His legs pushed his upper body, and his hands released the shot in rhythm with his extending arms. The ball traveled across the sky spinning toward destiny, Michael's eyes following every rotation.

Kathy and Danny were frozen in motion, watching. JP guided the ball with his eyes. Anthony and Lonzo watched the hoop as the ball traveled its last inches of its arc. And Sam kept his eyes on Michael. He was reading the entire moment off Michael's look of confidence. For Sam it would be a jinx if he did not trust Michael's face right now.

Swish! The ball dropped for the point.

Michael gave the clenched-fist power sign to John Paul.

Michael then said to him, "Yeah, JP! We did it! We all did it!" The boys were on Michael in an instant. Kathy and Danny stood in shock for a moment.

Danny finally spoke. "I can't believe it! Outrageous!"

Kathy had her hands to her face. "Oh, how sweet can it be-e-e!"

Danny put his arms around Kathy and gave her a bear hug that lifted her off the ground. "You crazy woman, you are wonderful."

After a moment he set her down.

She kept her arms around his neck and said, "So are you."

The boys rushed to their coaches. Congratulations went round and round.

Alyssum and her cheerleaders were still jumping with joy when Danny saw Chris and Poppi. They were watching the festivities from the safety of their seats. Danny could not believe his eyes. He waved to them and said, "I can't believe this."

Danny pushed his way through the crowd and got to them.

Poppi, in his wry way, said, "Think we'd let you have all the fun?"

Danny gave him a hug. "Well, no, but, how'd you find me?"

Poppi gestured to Chris. "My grandson. Smart boy."

Danny looked at Chris, who gave him five. Then Chris added, "Hot game, dad. Awesome."

Danny was speechless.

Poppi added, "Your boy here's been takin' care of me. Got rid of that housekeeper you hired. And, he's a damn good cook. Got that from me, of course."

Danny nodded and gave Chris a warm look. Had his boy finally come around? Whatever was going on was certainly a step in a good direction. A week ago, to see Poppi at this game and to know that Chris had taken care of him was unimaginable.

Poppi then insisted, "Go get your picture taken so we can go celebrate. My mouth's gettin' dry with all the smiles around here."

The comment made Danny's smile even bigger.

Danny rejoined his team and was pleased to see so many strangers
congratulating them. He looked at the excitement in each face, the
wonderful moment they would feel forever.

The awards ceremony took place on the field with those beautiful
mountains rising from the horizon. The three teams proudly stood
side by side on the colorfully decorated platform. The chief judge was
presenting the medals to each team member.

The boys were beaming with pride. Each one had their medal
hanging over their chest from a red, white and blue ribbon. Anthony,
Sam, Alonzo, John Paul and finally Michael each received the bronze
medallion.

The announcer spoke through the PA. "Let's hear it for the,
Hollywood Hawks. The 2005 bronze medal winners."

Kathy and Danny stood close by beaming with pride as the audience cheered and applauded. Danny looked toward the sky in a gesture of thanks.

Amid happy parents and others, Sanchez was applauding and
proudly talking with people around him, pointing to the Hawks.
Michael spotted him, and without hesitation, walked to him. Danny
noticed Michael and watched as he approached Sanchez.

Sanchez had his arms out as he said, "Congratulations, my son.
You must feel very proud."

Michael spoke honestly. "Not really."

"Que pasa?"

Michael handed Sanchez his medal. The old man admired it.

"Muy bonita." Sanchez handed it back, but Michael refused it.

"No. I want you to have it, Mr. Sanchez."

Sanchez looked at him for a long moment and then admired the medal again. "Thank you, Michael. This is about the money?"

"I needed it real bad, to help my mom. But I was only borrowing it. I'll pay you back, all of it. See, there wasn't enough with my pay. It was for the rent."

Sanchez scratched his chin. "All week long I say to myself, Antonio, why Michael no ask me?"

"I didn't know how to, Mr. Sanchez."

"But now you do?"

Michael was on the verge of tears. "I stole from you."

"I'm glad you realize that. More important, you know you stole from yourself." Sanchez looked at the medal again, then put it in Michael's hand. "I'll hold this after you come home. We make a work plan. Esta bien?"

Michael let a little smile of relief come through. "Yeah. Esta bien."

Sanchez reached forward and pulled the boy into his arms, giving him a strong hug. "So now you come back to work, I'll teach you to cook, just like my papa taught me."

"That'd be awesome."

"Bien. Awesome. Now, you go be with your friends. Go!" Sanchez brushed him away with a hand gesture.

Michael saw Alyssum, who was standing with her mother close by. He walked to them.

"Mom, this is Michael. He just won a bronze medal."

Janice put out her hand and shook his hard. "Michael, congratulations. You played a wonderful game. Beautiful medal."

"Thanks." Michael looked at the bronze medal again.

Janice then said, "I'll let you two talk," and joined other parents. Alyssum checked out the medal.

Michael asked, "Can I call you some time?"

Alyssum beamed at the question and handed him a note. "It's got my phone number."

He looked at it. "Three-ten. Had to be."

Over the loudspeakers the announcer called for the medalists to come together for a group picture. Michael looked over to the crowd and saw his team gathering.

He asked Alyssum, "Tonight? Can I call?"

She nodded cutely. "Now go get your picture taken."

He walked off toward the group. As the players assembled for the photograph, parents and friends were all smiles. They watched from behind the camera, taking in the warm sight of all the ecstatic boys. The pressure was over, and the members of those three teams were finally able to celebrate.

Kathy asked Danny, who was standing next to her, "Was that your dad?"

"That's Poppi and my boy. Can't believe it. It's the best. You can meet them—at dinner, tonight."

Kathy was surprised. She cocked her head, then grinned. "Only if it's Dutch treat," she said, laughing.

"You got it," he said.

"I'm kidding," she replied.

"No you weren't," he said. Then he laughed.

"Is this our first fight?" Kathy asked.

Laughing, they joined the boys just as Michael moved to John Paul, who held the game ball. He tossed it to Michael.

John Paul said, "Next year it's the gold."

"Nothin' less, JP."

Michael saw Chris, who gave him a thumbs up.

The photographer began setting up his shot. "Okay, everyone look this way."

The team, assembled and flanked by Kathy and Danny, was a study in enthusiasm. For a brief moment, Michael and JP could see Art standing with his cigar, proudly watching his boys. Then his image was gone.

The photographer was happy with the lineup and said, "On three."

Kathy and Danny exchanged a wink.

John Paul turned to Michael, raising his hand for a high-five. John Paul called out, "For Art!" Michael met his hand in the gesture.

All the boys said, "Yeah, Art!"

The photographer said, "One, two, three."

The camera strobe flashed and the photo was done. It would be a memory that each of the boys, Danny, and Kathy would have forever.

Was Art there? JP and Michael talked about it later and agreed, yes. Of course he was there. Art would stay with his boys till they made it past the playground and onto life.

But for now Art had to go. There were lots of other games yet to be played and he planned to see them all.